'I'm in no mo

'Are you in the m[...]
lowered his head a[...]
ing mouth and grac[...] long-
ing to float away on the blazing tide of
feelings he was arousing in her.

Finally, Charles laughed down at her, breathing hard.

'How dare you?' Lauren protested
ridiculously.

'You can't talk yourself out of what happened, Lauren. You resented it, but you sure
as hell responded.'

Dear Reader

Spring is here at last—a time for new beginnings and time, perhaps, finally to start putting all those New Year's resolutions into action! Whatever your plans, don't forget to look out this month for a wonderful selection of romances from the exotic Amazon, Australia, the Americas and enchanting Italy. Our resolution remains, as always, to bring you the best in romance from around the world!

The Editor

Alison York was born near Yorkshire's Moors and Dales but now lives in Warwickshire. A French graduate, she has two daughters and a son, all married, and two Siamese cats. She loves writing for the opportunity it offers to explore feelings and motivations. As well as novels, she writes short stories and poems. She is an avid reader—hell for her would have no books— and she also enjoys walking, gardening, theatre, music and art—other people's!

Recent titles by the same author:

DEAR ENEMY

FREE
TO LOVE

BY
ALISON YORK

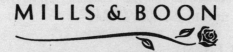

MILLS & BOON

MILLS & BOON LIMITED
ETON HOUSE, 18–24 PARADISE ROAD
RICHMOND, SURREY, TW9 1SR

MILLS & BOON and the Rose Device
are trademarks of the publisher.

First published in Great Britain 1995
by Mills & Boon Limited

© Alison York 1995

Australian copyright 1995   Philippine copyright 1995
This edition 1995

ISBN 0 263 78938 1

Set in 10 on 10½ pt Linotron Times
01-9504-61304

Typeset in Great Britain by Centracet, Cambridge
Made and printed in Great Britain

CHAPTER ONE

LAUREN was drawing Maggie's curtains up on the second floor of Allardyce House when the Lotus swept up the drive and crunched to a halt on the pebbles of the forecourt. She paused for a moment, looking down, curious to see what kind of a man was keeping her on duty late tonight with his last-minute reservation of a conference suite.

Long legs emerged from the low-slung car. A dark, immaculate head, broad shoulders. His back was towards her. He stretched briefly, then reached into the back of the car and took out a briefcase. He looked around, then began to turn, his head tilting as though to look up at the house. Perhaps he sensed that he was being watched. Lauren quickly stepped back and fully closed the curtains.

'Here, is he?' Maggie asked weakly from the bed. She was housemaid-cum-everybody's helper at the conference centre, and had just managed to get the Hampton Suite ready before giving in to a developing migraine.

'I presume it's him.' Lauren went over to the bed. 'Taken your tablet, Maggie?'

'You bet.'

'I'll see him settled, then as soon as the others arrive and his meeting's under way I'll run you home. Will you be all right until then?'

'No energy for getting into trouble! Sorry to be such a pain,' Maggie said. 'I could have walked, you know.'

'Right into the nearest tree, from the look of you! Close your eyes and let the magic pill do its work. I'll be back as soon as I can.' Lauren ran lightly downstairs

5

again, tucking in her shirt and smoothing her collar as she went.

He was standing in front of the reception desk, looking out into the grounds. A fawn cashmere overcoat hung loose from broad shoulders, his dark, crisply styled hair contrasting sharply with its muted colour. She had heard the ping of the desk bell as she ran downstairs, and he was reaching out to press it again as she spoke.

'Mr Lennox? Good evening. Welcome to Allardyce House.'

He turned, and she saw a strong, lean face. His eyes were riveting—a smoky green under emphatic dark brows. His firm jaw had the shadow of a strong but well-tamed beard.

'Good evening.' His voice was deep and attractive, his handshake firm. Lauren, not usually given to such thoughts, reflected briefly that if one had to work overtime, a client with looks like his afforded compensation. 'I was told this place was quiet and peaceful, but I was beginning to think it had more than a touch of the *Mary Celeste* about it,' he said.

Lauren smiled. 'There's no ghostly mystery about Allardyce House, thank goodness. Everything's ready for you. Would you like me to take your coat?'

He shrugged off his overcoat and handed it to her, revealing a dark grey suit of impeccable cut and fit, and a snowy white shirt, its collar sitting perfectly on the strong bronzed neck. The silk sheen and subtle pattern of his tie suggested the designer world. Lauren took the coat, its soft, luxurious cloth warm from his wearing of it, and placed it carefully over a chair.

'I'll hang it up when I've shown you the Hampton Suite.'

'It was fortunate that you could accommodate us.'

'I believe there was a fire at your original choice of venue?' she said as they walked towards the end of Reception.

'Only a small one, but as usual there was as much damage from putting the fire out as the fire itself caused.'

'Here we are.' Lauren held the door open. He was very tall. Her head didn't even come up to his shoulder.

The suite looked perfect. A rich clover-coloured carpet stretched from wall to wall, its colour echoed in the velvet curtains at the floor-to-ceiling windows. Good water-colours glowed against the plain cream walls, and a sparkling crystal chandelier hung over the polished mahogany surface of the conference table, around which comfortable chairs with padded seats and backs upholstered in dove-grey were arranged. There was the faint, delicious scent of old roses in the air from the pedestal arrangement between the two windows. No one could help but approve, Lauren thought with satisfaction.

Wrong. There was a slight frown of displeasure on the Lennox man's good-looking face as he turned towards her.

'I'm afraid this isn't at all what I asked for.'

'In what way, Mr Lennox? I wasn't on duty to take your original call. But if I can make any changes, I'll be glad to do so.'

'I asked for a setting appropriate to our numbers, since only three people are involved. And I was told that I would have complete privacy since this is a somewhat sensitive meeting. Glass doors opening into a public reception hall hardly fit that bill.'

Lauren was used to pouring oil on troubled waters left in her cousin Donna's wake. 'I can take the centre leaves out of the table and reduce it to a circle. Would that be more satisfactory?'

He shot back his cuff and looked pointedly at his watch. 'I hope there's time.'

'It won't take a moment.' Lauren worked rapidly and soon the table was re-set.

'Thank you. That's better,' he said briefly, getting papers out and distributing them round the table. But his eyes went again to the doors.

'We're not expecting anyone else tonight. Your party will be alone in Allardyce House, and entirely private,' Lauren assured him.

'You weren't expecting me, but I'm here,' he said pointedly. 'Do you have any kind of screen?'

'I believe we do. . .' Lauren said, not too enthusiastically. She was beginning to think that her initial impression of him had been based too much on face values.

'Then I'd be glad if you would have it brought in. I'm grateful for your help, but may I suggest that better lines of communication would be an improvement.'

Lauren murmured a conventional apology again but couldn't suppress a feeling of annoyance. Donna was so slipshod in the arrangements she made—this sort of thing happened all the time. But this man really had no grounds for being so niggly. He couldn't have contacted them much later in the day. He was lucky to be here at all. And the screen was up in an attic, probably with the dust of years on it. She ran up to the top floor and located it, dusted it off quickly, and lugged it down two flights of stairs before backing rather breathlessly through the glass doors.

With a muffled exclamation of disapproval, the Lennox man came round the table in quick strides and took the heavy screen from her.

'I expected you to send someone in with it, not risk injury by doing it yourself.'

'There doesn't happen to be anyone else here at the moment, Mr Lennox. It wasn't a problem, but thank you for your help.'

'Don't you have a man to do things like this?' She felt that he was aware of everything, from the flush of exertion to the cobweb on the cuff of her shirt which she had only just noticed herself.

'Yes. But he's not on duty tonight. If we'd had a little more notice of your meeting we would have made adequate staffing arrangements,' she said, looking calmly into the green eyes. Let him make what he wanted of that.

'You don't allow a margin for unforeseen circumstances? I think you should.'

'I believe I hear a car. That must be your guests.'

Thankfully she turned and went briskly through the doors to greet the rest of his party, hoping they would find favour more easily than Allardyce House had done, or it boded ill for the success of his meeting, whatever the nature of it might be.

Three men got out of the Bentley drawn up outside the main door, and Lauren showed them straight into the Hampton Suite.

She waited for a while until she was sure that the Lennox man wasn't going to discover some other omission to be rectified, then went up for Maggie.

Fortunately it was less than a five-minute run to Maggie's house, and Lauren was back in Reception putting the phone back on the hook in little more than ten minutes.

The indistinguishable murmur of voices in the Hampton Suite sounded peaceful enough. She sat down at her desk to deal with papers needed for the course scheduled to take place the following day.

She was a slight girl and, as she looked down at her work, the short, gamine cut of her silky raven-black hair emphasised the vulnerability of her slender neck and the elegant shape of her head. The light from the desk lamp gave warmth to creamy olive skin, and threw shadows on her cheek from long, dark lashes fringing expressive brown eyes.

She sighed imperceptibly, tired after ten consecutive days on duty, knowing that the coming weekend wouldn't provide much respite since she was due to attend a training exhibition at the NEC from Monday to Friday of the following week, and a week away would mean plenty of advance preparation to allow for her absence. Donna, her cousin and owner of Allardyce House, would see to that.

The Lennox man's criticism had been on the ball. They never had enough staff to feel comfortable at Allardyce House. Donna cut too many corners and relied far too much on everything going according to plan with no emergencies. That would have been all very well if Donna had been willing to roll up her own sleeves, but when something like tonight's last minute booking cropped up, she made sure that she herself was not inconvenienced. Her bridge evening had to go ahead as planned—the excuse being that it would be too much of a let-down for the other players if she cancelled. It was Lauren who had to drop everything and work on her night off, and other members of staff who had to put in the overtime while Donna swanned along in her self-absorbed way.

It was not going to go on like that, Lauren thought with determination as she switched on the word processor. Her own sweet, compliant mother had accepted it because she was eternally grateful to have been given a home at Allardyce House when she was expecting Lauren as a single parent. But she had paid for any favours done many times over during the years she had worked at the centre. In the numb period after her mother's death, Lauren seemed to have somehow slipped into taking her place on the staff, but she was not going to stay here for any longer than it took to get herself a decent job. Her mouth twisted wryly. If, it had to be said, anyone would take her on in the present climate on the strength of one unfinished business studies course, cut short by her mother's illness. Coming home to nurse her mother was something she had been determined to do, but she did regret her unachieved qualifications.

The garden beyond the open doors grew hazy in the dusk and the murmur of voices from the Hampton Suite rose and fell.

Mr Lennox had asked for a bottle of Bollinger to be chilled and ready, and at nine o'clock he rang for it to be brought in. Lauren sensed from the atmosphere that the meeting had gone well, and when she left the suite again the jovial male laughter now replacing the quiet businesslike hum confirmed it. At half-past nine they emerged, Charles Lennox going out to the car to see his guests off.

When he came back in, there was still a trace of his farewell smile transforming him so much that Lauren looked up and smiled at him.

'A successful meeting?' she asked.

'No comment at this stage.' Although he was smiling as he spoke, it seemed an unnecessary snub. She had not been asking for details, damn it, merely practising social politeness.

'You might ring through to the Beaufort and cancel the room in their garden extension that they offered me for tonight,' he went on, taking her by surprise. 'I'll stay here. It's late to move on. In any case, there's not likely to be much peace there tonight while they sort themselves out, I imagine.'

'I'm afraid you've been misinformed about the nature of this place, Mr Lennox,' she told him, rather pleased to be able to refuse him something legitimately. 'We're a conference centre, not a hotel. We don't take casual bookings.'

He frowned, then picked up a leaflet from the desk and read from it. 'It says here, "Residential Conference Centre". Residential suggests bedrooms. I'd like a bedroom. If people reside here, they must eat. I'd like food. Where's the problem?'

Lauren answered with her own brand of quiet firm-

ness, 'The problem is, Mr Lennox, that you made no
mention of meals or bedrooms when your late booking
was made. I understood that you merely wished to use
the conference suite for an evening meeting.'

'And now I want to use the other facilities offered
here in print by Allardyce House.' He tapped the
leaflet smartly. 'Is it too much of a challenge for this
place to provide cold meat and salad. . .a bit of fresh
fruit? I'm not asking for a banquet.' His eyes went
deliberately to the car park. 'I hardly think your rooms
are all taken. Well? Are they?'

'No,' she said reluctantly. They were all empty, as
anyone could deduce from the fact that his Lotus was
the only car on the forecourt.

'Are they required for other people early tomorrow
morning?'

'We have a course for fourteen people here
tomorrow.'

'A residential course?'

He didn't miss a trick. Lauren coloured slightly,
caught out.

'No. A day course,' she said shortly.

'Then my sleeping in one of your rooms can't create
any insurmountable problems.'

Lauren thought of the chef who lived out and
probably would be unable to be contacted tonight
since he wasn't expecting to have to provide any meals
until lunch tomorrow, then of Maggie's migraine.

'I really haven't the authority to go against house
policy,' she said.

'Then I suggest you contact someone who has.' The
green eyes stared implacably at her, stonewalling all
opposition. 'I'll collect up my things while you sort
something out.'

He went back into the Hampton Suite, and Lauren,
feeling decidedly ruffled, made for the kitchen to ring
Donna in privacy.

'What's all this about?' her cousin asked when

summoned to the phone, none too pleased to have her game interrupted.

Lauren told her. 'He's going to be pretty stroppy if he's thwarted—he's that sort of person,' she said.

'The deciding factor's whether he might be good for more business, then. What do you think?'

'At a guess, I'd say he's quite a big fish.' Lauren's tone was reluctant, but she added with more feeling, 'He seems to think he is, anyway.'

'Then it's obvious: we let him have a room. No point in turning away good money and antagonising a future customer.'

'Any particular room you'd like me to put him in?'

'Oh, use your initiative, for heaven's sake!' Donna said impatiently, and put the phone down.

Lauren ran upstairs and checked the most impressive of the centre's bedrooms, annoyed with herself to be offering him the best, but he was the kind of man who made that the automatic option, then hurried down again.

'All arranged?' he asked, coming through the glass doors with his briefcase, obviously not expecting any other outcome.

Lauren swallowed her irritation. 'Yes, Mr Lennox. I'm authorised to make an exception in this particular case.'

He looked down at her and satisfaction flickered in the green eyes. 'I rather thought that your proprietor would be willing to make a rational compromise.'

Lauren swallowed the urge to retort with difficulty. 'If you follow me, I'll show you to your room.'

'One moment. I'll bring in my case.' He returned with an expensive-looking Gucci suitcase and refused her offer to take it with a firm, 'Certainly not.'

She led him up to the room, which overlooked the Italian garden at the side of the house. He looked round and went over to stare out of the window into the quiet darkness of the grounds before turning and

saying, 'At least I shall have peace and quiet for the
work I have to do before a one o'clock meeting
tomorrow. And before alarm bells ring—I expect to
be billed for two nights since I shall be needing this
place beyond what I presume is the ten o'clock
deadline.'

'Very well, Mr Lennox.' Lauren went over to draw
the curtains and light the lamps. When she turned
round he had removed both tie and jacket and was
rolling up his shirt-sleeves, revealing brown muscular
arms, the dark hair on his chest in the open neck of his
shirt a sudden, earthy contrast to the snowy white. She
was surprised by a strong stirring of response to his
masculinity. She was not the sort of girl who fancied
men indiscriminately—too much about her life proved
the folly of that. He had hardly been out to charm her
since he'd walked into Allardyce House. And yet she
was reacting to him in a way that she found profoundly
disturbing. She took quick refuge in routine patter.

'The bathroom is through the door on your right.
Your meal will be ready in the dining-room in half an
hour. We could, of course, provide a hot meal, but it
would take a little longer.' Although she hadn't the
slightest desire to please him she found herself pro-
voked to try. What was happening to her?

His patient dismissal of the offer was as good as a
cold shower. 'As I said, a salad is all I need. I had a
heavy lunch. I'll be down in half an hour.'

Wishing she had offered him arsenic or ground glass,
Lauren went downstairs. In the kitchen she took off
her suit jacket and resigned herself to becoming, after
receptionist and chambermaid, *chef de cuisine*.

Well before the half-hour was up she was waiting in
the dining-room with a window table attractively laid
and lamplit, and a silver dish of ham and turkey cut
fresh from the bone on a side table, along with a bowl
of salad that managed to look as though care and
artistry and not speed had been essential in its cre-

ation. Crusty rolls, both brown and white, hot from the oven, smelled deliciously appetising.

Charles Lennox came in and she watched him walk towards her down the length of the dining-room. If the dining-room had been full, heads would have turned with interest as he passed, Lauren thought. She herself was watching him far too obviously, she realised with a start, turning to pull back his chair.

'There's asparagus soup or avocado vinaigrette if you would like a starter?' she suggested as he sat down.

'Nothing more than I've already ordered,' he said dismissively, but he disarmed her almost immediately with an expression of genuine pleasure as she brought over the main course. 'Ah! That looks good——' He looked up at her, the smoky-green of his eyes more startling than ever at close quarters '—though this non-stop personal service you provide in all areas becomes a little disconcerting. Should I be flattered?'

'I'm sure you're no stranger to good service, Mr Lennox,' she said briefly. 'Would you like to see the wine list?'

'No. I'll finish off the Bollinger.' She had already put it in a champagne bucket beside him. 'And I wouldn't mind a bottle of mineral water.'

When she brought it, he had already started his meal. 'Rather more than I thought,' he said, lifting the champagne bottle slightly in the bucket. 'Would you like a glass?'

'Thank you, but I never drink on duty,' Lauren said.

'Even on duty for one client?' he said disbelievingly.

She looked at him, unabashed. 'The rule still stands.'

The dark eyebrows rose. 'I assure you that the offer was made "without prejudice", as they say.'

She gave a slight smile. 'So was the refusal.'

There was a flicker of something that could have

been amusement in his eyes. He nodded in the direction of the strawberries and cream on the side table.

'I presume those are for me?'

'They are. And there's a cheese platter under the cover, though I am aware that you didn't ask for it,' she told him pointedly, remembering his ungracious rejection of a first course.

'Perhaps I shall redeem myself with cheese and biscuits, then,' he said solemnly. Lauren blushed, and instantly felt quite ridiculous. He gave a low laugh and went on, 'I suggest you run along and leave me to look after myself. I think that would be more acceptable for both of us. I'll ring down for coffee from my room when I'm back upstairs.'

'Very well, Mr Lennox,' she said stiffly. 'Enjoy your meal.'

While he ate, she prepared the conference-room for the following day, restoring the table to its full size and putting out extra chairs. She found herself thinking more than she liked about Charles Lennox. When he had smiled just now, he had looked completely different. His mouth had revealed itself as surprisingly sensual, his eyes as having warm, even exciting depths. Moreover, he had suddenly looked vaguely familiar, and she couldn't think why because she knew that they had never met before. Her mind brooded about him, teased by the conundrum, and once she heard him go back upstairs she was strangely on edge until he rang down for his coffee. She found her attitude puzzling. She was used to dealing with all kinds of men around the centre. Why should this particular one make her feel so unsettled? And why on earth couldn't he have had his coffee in the dining-room? she thought irritably as she climbed the stairs with the heavy tray.

He was hard at work, papers spread under the lamplight on the desk when she opened the door of his bedroom in response to his preoccupied, 'Come in.' Again she experienced that instant flash of awareness

of his rugged physical attractiveness. The light emphasised the healthy sheen of his hair, deepened the tan
on his arms below the shirt-sleeves which he had once
again pushed up, cast shadows that emphasised the
bone-structure of his face.

'Just put it here,' he told her absently, patting the
desk. Then he realised who she was and looked up in
surprise. 'You again. Does anybody do any work
around here apart from you?'

'Quite a few people,' she said quietly.

'Then where are they all?'

'Off duty. As I said downstairs, Mr Lennox, we are
not a hotel and we don't function in the same way. We
organise our staffing according to prearranged bookings. Yours didn't fall into that category.'

'What you are saying, politely disguised, is that the
non-prearranged clients are a hell of a nuisance, I
suppose?' he said, tipping back on his chair, his green
eyes looking steadily at her.

'No.' She looked at him with heightened colour,
wondering why on earth she was bothering to be polite
to this man. Her legs ached, her head ached, and it
would have been rather satisfying to empty the coffee-
pot over his head. 'Do you think you have any cause
for complaint, Mr Lennox? Because if so, I'll say
without any polite disguise whatsoever that I couldn't
disagree with you more. You came here as an eleventh-
hour booking, and your every wish has been met to
the best of my ability. You have even been given a
room and a meal in direct contravention of house
policy. I'm rather at a loss to think what more can be
done to meet with your approval. Will there be anything else?' It sounded more like a threat than an offer
of help.

'What would I dare request?' he said, now openly
amused. 'The quixotic nature of this place indicates
that if I asked for a bit of relaxing female company,

you'd probably turn up in that capacity as well as the rest.'

'That's a cheap gibe,' Lauren said coldly.

'Merely an extension of Allardyce House logic as I see it.'

She turned on her heel and took a step towards the door, but he seized her wrist and halted her, making her look at him as his hard fingers gripped her.

'You're tired, aren't you?' he said, studying her face.

'Yes. What's your excuse?' she returned, quick as a flash.

'May I suggest that your anger should be directed against an employer who forces you to work under such inadequate conditions? The choice is yours, surely? If you don't like the heat, you get out of the kitchen. As for myself—I don't need an excuse. The customer is always right. Didn't anybody ever teach you that?'

'Learning the theory is easy. Putting it into practice at times would try the patience of a saint.'

'And you're no saint?'

'I think I've demonstrated that.'

'I think we both have.' He released her wrist. 'I shall want nothing else tonight. And to smooth your ruffled feathers, I shall not want breakfast tomorrow. I see there are the usual drinks-making things. Instant coffee's all I shall have time for in the morning.' He smiled at her suddenly, and as suddenly as her anger had erupted it subsided under that unexpectedly warm, transforming smile. But he was still holding her wrist. She looked pointedly at his hand.

'Off you go, then,' he said, releasing her.

'We don't keep a night porter,' she told him with as much calmness as she could muster, 'so I'm afraid there will be no one on duty until seven o'clock tomorrow morning.'

'I didn't dream for one moment that there would be,' he said ironically.

'You will find a list of emergency numbers and other information next to the telephone.'

'I shall endeavour not to use them.'

'It's merely a matter of house policy to draw attention to them. Goodnight, Mr Lennox.'

'Goodnight. . .' His eyes went to the neat name badge she wore on her lapel, then back to hold hers for a moment. 'Goodnight, Miss Frazer.' Was he seeing her as a person for the first time, or memorising her name for any complaints he might decide to make? The latter, most likely.

Well. . .nought out of ten for that little encounter, Lauren thought bemusedly as she went downstairs again. She couldn't remember ever being so openly rude to a client before, but the Lennox man had needled her beyond bearing. Not merely needled her, if she was honest. She had never before felt so. . .so affected by a man. It was as though he could arouse any emotion in her that he chose. Anger, the wish to give way to physical violence and ill-considered verbal retort—and at the other end of the scale, the desire to please and the kind of physical response that, she knew only too well from her mother's experience, led to danger. Head first, heart after, she had vowed would be her approach to men. Unfortunately, in this case, neither her head nor her heart appeared to be obeying the rules. She worked her shoulders to get rid of the tension in them. There were still things to do for tomorrow's course. She had better forget the man.

It was half-past eleven before Donna drifted in just as Lauren was finishing some photocopying. Her cousin, who seemed exhausted by her evening's pleasure, invited Lauren to come into the kitchen for coffee while they went through what had been happening at the centre, so it was almost midnight before Lauren was able to drop the latch on the main door as

she went out and headed for the Lodge which had
been home for the whole of her twenty-three years.

There was a full moon, but all the same Lauren had
not seen the figure standing in a gap in the trees at the
edge of the birch copse she had to go through until the
cracking of a twig drew her attention and made her
stop in her tracks, momentarily alarmed.

'Did I startle you?' a voice which she recognised
with an equal mixture of thankfulness and unease as
Charles Lennox's asked, as he looked over his
shoulder.

'You did rather. I had no idea you'd come out.'

'I had a head full of figures and wanted to get rid of
them before settling down. Which way does the motorway lie? It looks so peaceful out there I can hardly
believe it exists.'

Lauren stepped reluctantly over to his side. 'To the
right. That fold of land hides it from view.'

The landscape was bathed in moonlight. At that
moment, the unmistakable mating cry of a vixen rang
out.

'What the hell was that?' he exclaimed.

'A vixen,' Lauren said, not elaborating.

'Ah!' There was instant comprehension in his tone.
Lauren was aware as he spoke that he was looking
down at her. 'I suppose it is that kind of a night. . .'

The sharp rustle of leaves under her feet emphasised
her hurry to get away from him.

'Did you bring your keys with you?' She was conscious of her voice being a tone higher than it should
have been.

'No. Since I'm the only guest, it seemed pointless to
lock my room.' He sounded mildly amused. That
helped.

'But it *is* necessary to have the other key on your
ring in order to get back into the house at this time of
night. I didn't know you had gone out. I locked the
door as I left.'

'This really is a one-horse establishment you're running here, isn't it?' He didn't sound quite so amused now. 'Surely there's someone I can knock up? I heard a car drive up a little while ago.'

Lauren wished him at the other end of the earth. 'It won't be necessary to disturb anyone. I'll walk back with you and let you in.' She added with a certain asperity, 'If you had referred to the information near the telephone in your room, you would have read the clause about keys.'

'I didn't get round to it, obviously. I too have had an extremely busy day.' They headed towards the edge of the copse. 'You don't live in, then?' he asked.

'No. But I live quite close.'

'I should hope so, if you make a habit of walking home at this time of night. From the way you work, I'd guess this is a family partnership. Am I right?'

'The proprietor is my cousin. I work for her.'

'I see. A subtle distinction. I hope you get your hands on some of the profits for your Herculean labours, Miss Frazer.'

Lauren quickened her pace. 'No comment, Mr Lennox. I don't discuss business with outsiders.'

He laughed at her huffiness. 'In my line of work, it's second nature to spot the weaknesses in every concern I visit, and the weaknesses at Allardyce House are glaringly obvious.' They were passing a seat, and he stopped her, his hand firm on her arm. 'Sit down for a moment. People queue up to pay for my advice, but as I've caused you a certain amount of trouble, it's yours for nothing.'

'I don't want to sit down, and this is no time of day to listen to advice,' Lauren said, exasperated. 'It's midnight, and I have the not unreasonable wish to get home and go to bed.'

'Two minutes. No more.'

His insistent pressure on her arm and the fact that the back of her knees suddenly came up against the seat combined to force her to do as he wished. She sat stiffly, inwardly fuming.

'Allardyce House is charming. It is tastefully decorated and furnished. The grounds are attractive, and the place is ideally situated. But the way it's run is sadly inadequate.' Lauren tensed and would have got up but he retained his grip on her arm and prevented her doing so. 'Tell your cousin that the impression of being run on a shoestring is a killer. She should hire adequate staff, or give up. If she really means business she should convert the stable block I saw from my room behind the house to a single-room student area and keep the main house for top management and general hotel accommodation. This nonsense about not taking casual bookings must irritate others as well as myself. Tell her above all that having a tame relative who looks like an angel, almost but not quite has the patience of a saint, and seems to be capable of doing anything, just isn't enough. How much more is expected of you, for heaven's sake? You were doing accounts when I arrived this evening, and I see from the board outside the Hampton Suite that Miss Lauren Frazer is running tomorrow's office management course.'

'Which I am perfectly capable of doing,' Lauren protested defensively. 'I spent three years at one of the north's most respected business colleges.'

'I don't doubt your capability. But are you telling me that you have a degree in business studies and allow yourself to be exploited as chambermaid, scullery maid and general dogsbody in a rural backwater like this? You must be crazy.'

'I don't have a degree. I had to leave before finals because of personal circumstances.' She glared at him, almost quivering with indignation, and realising that she was telling him far more than she wished. 'I hope you are more tactful with people who pay for your advice.'

'I don't deal in tact. I go in for plain speaking.' He stood. 'And, having spoken plainly, that's it. Expert advice, and yours for nothing.'

'And now I presume I may open the door?' Lauren said furiously, springing to her feet, her fury all the stronger because his assessment of the situation at Allardyce House was so shrewdly accurate.

'Take my advice,' he said, pausing beside her in the doorway. 'If you can't talk sense into this operation, get out.'

It took every shred of Lauren's will-power to answer him politely. 'I didn't ask for any advice, Mr Lennox,' she said. 'And now I'll wish you goodnight.'

'Think about it,' he told her relentlessly before the door closed.

As always, the charm and comfort of the home she and her mother had created worked its healing magic as she relaxed against the cool chintz of the sofa. Lauren could remember the Lodge as a bare and even ramshackle place in her childhood, but little by little over the years treasure-hunts through auction sales had come up with furniture that harmonised perfectly with the old house. Their tight budget had been miraculously stretched to pay for paint, wallpapers and furnishing fabrics whose subtle, pale colours enhanced the reduced light that came into the rooms through the small, diamond-paned windows. There was hardly ever a moment of the year when bowls of something fresh and colourful from Anne Frazer's garden could not be seen on the shelves and tables. Whatever annoyances might arise in Allardyce House, here was peace and security. This was *home*.

But working at Allardyce House was certainly not what Lauren had planned. She thumped a cushion in renewed anger. She didn't need anyone else to tell her that. She knew that she was being exploited, just as her mother had been exploited.

The little grandmother clock chimed half-past midnight. As she got up and began the nightly winding-down chores, there was a determined set to her mouth, a warning brightness in her eyes.

In my own time and in my own way I shall sort out my life, she promised herself. Herself? At the back of her mind she knew that she was addressing a man with unforgettable green eyes, eyes that apparently saw both what was there to be seen, and what had to be deduced. . .

CHAPTER TWO

NEXT morning, sunny as the day in a corn-coloured suit with pleated skirt and collarless jacket, Lauren was halfway to Allardyce House at eight o'clock when she saw Charles Lennox running towards her.

He began to speak before he reached her, his breathing unaffected by the run, nor was there any glistening of sweat on forehead or throat—just the glow of superb fitness.

'Put forest bark down on this path and erect appropriate signs and you've got a running track. An asset there for the taking! Good morning!' The last two words he apparently threw in as an afterthought.

'A new day, and new ideas so early in it, Mr Lennox!' she observed coolly as he ran past her. 'Do you never stop?'

'It doesn't pay. Ever looked at stagnant water?' he called crisply over his shoulder.

Lauren only caught one more brief glimpse of him as she came through Reception at the end of the morning session of her course. He was immaculately dressed for business again, and deep in conversation with Donna, who was looking up into his face with avid attention, hanging on every word. Lauren gave them a wide berth as she headed for the Lodge, where she always took lunch on course days to give herself a break.

It was only by chance that she went into the sitting-room when she had eaten her ready-prepared salad in the kitchen. The glass door to the garden was wide open, and Lauren knew that she had checked that all was secure before she left for the main house earlier in the day. She frowned, then closed and locked it, and went on a quick tour of the house checking on its contents. Nothing appeared to be missing. All the same, it was the sort of discovery that left an uneasy feeling.

Back in Allardyce House she stopped to report what had happened. Donna reacted oddly by going rather pink in the face.

'Oh—how careless of me. I was over there earlier on. I didn't realise I'd left the door open. Don't worry. You haven't had a prowler.'

Lauren was taken aback. In all the time she had been living there, she had never known either her aunt or her cousin come into the house uninvited. Her unspoken question must have been plainly written on her face.

'Nothing to worry about,' Donna said, regaining her composure. 'I just wanted to have a look round before I dealt with the insurance. It occurred to me that since you and Aunt Anne have been living there, it's rather a different place from when we first had it assessed. I think it would be as well to have it officially inspected again.'

'I see,' Lauren said briefly, thinking it wouldn't have hurt Donna to ask before barging in.

'I know I should have asked, but you were busy, weren't you? And if I don't do things when I think of them they get forgotten.'

'Well, rather you than a stranger,' Lauren said, then, fearing that she might have sounded as ungracious as she felt, she added, 'So that's all right then. Has the Lennox man gone?'

Donna blushed again at the name. He must have made quite an impression. 'Oh, yes. He left before one. Some meeting or other.' She looked at the clock. 'Time you were back with the course, isn't it? There's a pile of correspondence for you to do when you've finished. I don't want too much left to cope with next week while you're away. And you don't mind working on Sunday when we have the Golden Wedding party in, do you? Maggie's still a bit rough and she could do with the weekend off.'

And Maggie would have to be paid, whereas Lauren's salary remained at its modest level no matter how many hours it was stretched to cover. Lauren gave a resigned nod. 'I'll be around, Donna.'

'Good. You'll have Saturday to get yourself ready for next week, once the duplicating for the Wednesday group is done.' In masterly fashion Donna slipped in another extra.

'If you can't stand the heat, get out of the kitchen.' The Lennox man's words entered Lauren's mind unbidden. She frowned at the intrusion. She knew Donna took advantage of her. She didn't need some outsider to tell her that. She dismissed him unceremoniously and headed for the conference suite.

It had been a tiring but exhilarating week at the training exhibition. Dying for a cup of tea, and knowing that if she went straight to Donna there was sure to be some job waiting to welcome her back, Lauren left her mother's little blue Mini in the quiet lane beyond the old drive gates, and cut through the hedge to the Lodge.

She let herself in with the little glow of pleasure the house always gave her and went straight through into the sitting-room to open windows before putting the kettle on.

But windows were forgotten as she came to an abrupt halt in the doorway. Her furniture had been moved, and, she realised with increasing alarm, her personal photographs were missing. Another absence registered—the delicate mahogany plant-stand that always stood in the bay window was nowhere to be seen. It was one of the last auction purchases she and her mother had made, and as such had special sentimental value. In its place was a desk with a lap-top computer and a pile of stationery on it.

It could only be Donna. Anger began to build up in Lauren. Tea was forgotten as she embarked on a tour of the Lodge to see what other changes her cousin had seen fit to make. The kitchen seemed its usual self. So did the hall. She ran upstairs and into her bedroom. All was well there too. But how long would it stay that way now Donna had embarked on invading her cousin's territory?

Angrily Lauren went over to slide back the wardrobe door with the intention of taking out a pair of jeans and a T-shirt to change into. Like a jack-in-the-box, another startling surprise leapt out at her, rooting her to the spot. Instead of hangers of her own colourful feminine clothes, a row of more sober male suits, shirts and pullovers met her eyes. She had barely time to wonder what on earth was going on when she heard a key in the lock of the front door. The door opened, closed again, then there were leisurely footsteps going through the hall.

Lauren's normally full, sweet mouth tightened, then her eyes grew bright with purpose as she tiptoed across the bedroom floor and went silently down the stairs to give her cousin as big and as unpleasant a surprise as she had had herself.

She only got as far as the sitting-room doorway before the world went suddenly black as something was flung over her head, while arms like iron bands killed at birth any attempt to drag the blanket or whatever it was away from her face. A man's voice was saying, muffled by the folds of the thing that was nearly suffocating her, 'Oh no, you don't! We'll have you through here, where you can't make a run for the door. And then we'll see just who you are.'

This time she had not even considered the possibility of an intruder, but now she panicked and fought like a wildcat, kicking and attempting to head-butt whoever

was dragging her into the sitting-room. She heard him
swear, and found herself thrown on to her side on the
settee, where he managed to anchor both her arms
behind her back, and sat on her legs. She had never
been more afraid in her life, and never more
powerless.

'Now!' she heard him say, his voice still indistinct,
but the anger in it unmistakable. 'We'll see whose little
hellcat you happen to be.'

She had no time to puzzle over the words. One of
his hands held both her wrists in a vice-like grip. The
other pulled away the rug, and simultaneous excla-
mations burst from attacker and attacked.

'You!'

'You!'

Lauren found herself staring up at Charles Lennox,
whose hair was roughed up and whose tie was askew.
The rug turned out to be an overcoat, a familiar pale
cashmere overcoat. Surprise made him relax his grip
on her hands, and she instantly shot upright and thrust
at him with all her strength.

'Get off my legs! You're breaking them!'

'You're lucky I didn't break your neck,' he said
ungraciously, darting a malevolent look at her, but he
moved aside and she swung her legs on to the floor.

'Who on earth did you imagine I was?' she said
breathlessly, rubbing hard at her legs to get the circulation going again.

'Someone eager to get enough information to under-
cut me on an important deal.'

'How ridiculous!'

'Industrial espionage happens. What the hell are you
doing in here, anyway?' he asked.

Lauren sat up and stared at him in outrage. 'You
ask *me* that?'

'I expressly stated that I wished no staff—cleaning
or otherwise—to come into the Lodge during the

period I'm here,' he went on. 'You were busybodying around upstairs, weren't you?'

Lauren couldn't believe her ears. 'I *beg* your pardon?'

'You heard me perfectly clearly. But if you want time to think up an excuse, I'll say it again. This house is out of bounds to all staff, including your cousin and yourself, while I am renting it.'

'Renting it?' Lauren croaked disbelievingly, feeling as though she had been punched in the stomach.

An expression of bored enlightenment settled on his face. 'Don't tell me! The wonderful system broke down again. You didn't know I was taking over the Lodge. Is there no communication in this place?'

Lauren was struggling to take in what he had said. His out-of-the-blue attack on her had been shock enough. This was worse. Renting the Lodge? Taking over her home? She couldn't believe it. Didn't want to believe it. How could Donna do this to her?

'I've been away,' she said weakly.

He gave a scornful snort. 'That much was quite obvious. To put it mildly, Allardyce House has not been running on oiled wheels during your absence. But I don't suppose that surprises you.'

'Tell me what's going on. I haven't spoken to Donna. I'm only just back.' Her thoughts were running round in wild circles.

'Business is going on. Business that brings me to this area, sensitive business. I'm dealing with it from this house, and I don't wish anyone—that goes for you and your cousin as well as the rest of your staff—to come in and out of the place while I am here. I am perfectly capable of taking care of myself, and my prime requirement is absolute privacy. Is that understood?' Suspicion clouded his eyes again. 'What exactly *were* you doing in here, in any case?'

Lauren was beginning to realise that he couldn't be

speaking to her like this if he knew that the Lodge was her home and he had turned her out of it. She felt totally humiliated by the situation, and it would be even more humiliating to be the one who made Charles Lennox aware of the true position.

'I noticed the bedroom window open,' she said, inventing rapidly. 'We have to be particularly careful about security at the Lodge since it is such a long way from the main house.'

'Then if that's the excuse for the intrusion, I'll make sure no windows are left open in future.' His eyes narrowed. 'Where else have you been? In this room?'

'I checked everywhere, naturally.'

'Including the papers on my desk?'

Lauren flushed. 'Your papers are no concern of mine, Mr Lennox. I assure you that I wouldn't dream of looking through them.'

'I'm glad to hear it,' he said curtly. He made an exaggerated gesture towards the door. 'Then if you've quite recovered from the surprise of finding me here, I won't detain you any further. I have things to do, and I'm sure you have too. I hope there are no ill effects from our little encounter.'

Thus dismissed from her own home, Lauren felt a tremendous urge to thump him right on his aristocratic-looking nose.

'Little encounter?' she snarled. 'Were you ever in the SAS?'

He grinned, infuriating her further. 'No. But I'm flattered that you think I could have been.'

'Don't be. It wasn't intended as a compliment.' Still she couldn't believe this situation. 'Why the Lodge?' she asked in desperation.

'Because it's secluded, convenient and, for the length of time I shall be using it, quite tolerable.'

Lauren seethed to hear her home spoken of in such a disparaging way.

'High praise indeed!' she said cuttingly, and without another word turned and left the house before she exploded.

Once in her car, she was hit by the reaction she had been forced to suppress and her hands were shaking so much that she had difficulty inserting the key in the ignition.

Her home. . .Donna had taken her home away from her without a word. That she could do such a thing was unspeakably hurtful. She should be made to answer for it right away.

Donna was quite unrepentant. She began by stating that good business simply couldn't be turned away. In time-honoured fashion, she then lost her temper and reminded Lauren that the Lodge was not hers and never would be, and that by occupying it she prevented her cousin and employer from benefiting from the little gold mine she now knew it to be. The use of the place—and of Lauren's furniture, for two short weeks, she said, steely-eyed—was scant repayment for twenty-two years of rent-free accommodation.

All this was undeniably true. What could Lauren say in answer to such cold logic? She was informed that she was relegated to the staff floor in the main house, where the redecorating of Allardyce House had stopped short, leaving a residue of dingy thirties wallpapers, all browns and dull greens, and cheerless as winter.

Still scarcely believing what was happening, Lauren made her way to the depressing little room under the eaves. The contents of her kitchen cupboards had been deposited in open cardboard boxes along one wall. Her clothes hung on a rickety tidy-rail in front of the food boxes. The photographs were crowded together on the high windowsill, and the plant-stand was squashed in between a shabby chest of drawers and the narrow bed.

'I know it won't achieve miracles,' Maggie said

laconically appearing in the open doorway, 'but I've made some tea. And I've emptied a cupboard in the staff kitchen if you want to get rid of the Harvest Festival atmosphere in here.'

Lauren managed a smile. 'Thanks, Maggie. Tea's just what I'm dying for. But you should be home now.'

'I hung around to put it on record that I only did what I was told to do, moving all your things,' Maggie said bluntly.

'I guessed that.'

'I had a feeling you didn't know anything about it. One look at your face now tells me I was right. What a homecoming!'

'Life's never short of surprises. Let's have that tea. How've you been?' Tempting though it was at this moment to say exactly what she thought about her cousin's behaviour, Lauren firmly changed the subject. Never discuss the family with the staff, her mother had instilled into her, and the habit of a lifetime prevailed.

Maggie refused the offer of tea, and hung on to the subject. 'It wouldn't be so bad if you hadn't had such a load of trouble with that Lennox man. It really puts the icing on the cake, doesn't it, to think of him in your house?'

'It wouldn't have made much difference whoever took over the Lodge, I suppose,' Lauren said, but without conviction.

'You said you thought you had seen him before. I found a bit about him in the paper when I was lighting the fire.' Maggie fished a newsprint photograph out of her pocket and gave it to Lauren. 'Don't suppose you'll like him any better for what you read there. Don't suppose you want to, either! Oh, well, tomorrow's another day. Chuck the cutting when you've read it. So long, Lauren.'

'Bye, Maggie. Thanks for the tea.' Lauren's eyes were already scanning the sensational headline over the picture of a smiling Charles Lennox. 'Get lost, sweetheart!' the tabloid-speak blazed. 'Eligible city tycoon Charles Lennox leaves yet another bride-to-be waiting at the church, as near as dammit. Less than a week before the knot was to be tied at one of London's most sought-after wedding venues, "It's off!" announces the groom. Sounds familiar? It should. Imogen Carpenter isn't the first pretty angler to find Charles Lennox a hard fish to land.'

Lauren read to the end of the unsavoury article. It sounded as though the Lennox man was the kind she had most cause to be wary of. The same type as her father, who had wanted all the fun and none of the responsibility—and who had turned her mother and his inconvenient unborn child out of his life without a second thought. She screwed up the scrap of newsprint and threw it into the bin. One whole week more he would be here, taking over her territory. And she could do nothing, absolutely nothing, about it except put on her public face and grin and bear it.

But Maggie was wrong in thinking she would be glad to read such unpleasantness. She had a strange sense of let-down. . .strange, because why should she care that the man putting her out of her home should have a reputation like this? And yet somehow she did.

Her disillusionment and anger, though of necessity suppressed, affected the tone of her next encounter with Charles Lennox when he came into Reception on Monday.

'A gold pen I'm particularly fond of is missing,' he said. 'I last used it on Friday. You didn't happen to notice it when you were in the Lodge?'

Rightly or wrongly, she read accusation in the green eyes. Lauren's colour rose. 'If you are entertaining suspicions that I might have taken a fancy to it, let me disillusion you at once. I didn't attempt to steal information from you, nor did I make off with your pen. In fact, I would find a gold pen too much of a responsibility—and just a touch ostentatious.'

There was no trace of embarrassment on his face. 'Are you still bearing a grudge for Friday? It was a genuine mistake.'

'No, I'm not bearing a grudge,' Lauren said untruthfully. 'I am reacting to what seems like an unpleasant accusation.'

'If I had reason to make accusations, I would do so directly.' The strong eyebrows rose. 'Are you always so touchy? I merely came over to report a loss, not a theft.'

Again Charles Lennox had succeeded in provoking a spontaneous and, according to him, wrong reaction. 'No member of staff has been over to the Lodge,' she said, deciding to stick to her guns in spite of him. 'And in any case, they're all completely honest.'

'I'm not accusing your staff either, but I'm reassured by your faith in them.'

'I was leading up to offering to send someone over to search the Lodge,' she offered frostily.

He brushed aside the offer. 'I don't want anyone over there, remember?'

She could have kicked herself. Who better than she to remember his antipathy to visitors? 'Then there doesn't seem much I can do about it,' Lauren said, turning back to her word processor.

A hand slammed down on the keyboard, hopelessly fouling up the screen. 'You could listen for a moment, if that's possible.' The green eyes looked with glacial authority into hers. She swallowed, and listened. 'If the pen turns up after I have gone, I would be most grateful to have it returned to me at this address.' He put a business card, reverse side up, on the desk in front of her, pointing to the hand-written address—a village ten miles or so away—on the back of it. His eyes met hers again. 'That's all. It needn't have taken all this time to get the message across.'

'I'll make sure whoever deals with the Lodge knows to look out for the pen,' Lauren said, deciding that no response to that was the safest option as she put the card away in the corner of the top drawer of her desk.

'And as far as the question of ostentation goes,' he added, surprising her, 'I don't give tuppence for the fact that the pen is gold. It's important to me because of the person who gave it to me.'

Lauren's eyes fell in embarrassment. 'I hope it turns up.'

'So do I. I also hope that your day improves as it progresses. Good morning, Miss Frazer.'

My house! Lauren wanted to call after him. It's my house you're staying in, my house you're losing your stupid pen in, you insufferable, big-headed, sarcastic man. She didn't say it, of course. She got her head down over her work, but she attacked it as ferociously as she would have liked to attack Charles Lennox.

Perhaps it was a small prick of conscience that made Donna take advantage of lack of business to give Lauren an unexpected morning off on Wednesday. She was on her way out of the main door when she met Charles Lennox on his way in.

'I want a word with you,' he said.

'I'm not on duty this morning, Mr Lennox. Donna is around.'

'But it's you I want to speak to. Going out for a walk?'

Since she was wearing jeans, a thick jersey and scarf, and her favourite soft hiking boots, it was fairly obvious.

'Yes,' she said briefly and unhelpfully.

'Then I'll not hold you up. I'll walk with you a little way.'

Lauren found herself reluctantly heading down the drive by his side. The reason he wanted to speak to her was soon made obvious. He took three envelopes from his pocket and held them out to her.

'Your post, I believe.'

Lauren took it from him with a brief word of thanks. The postman had been told to deliver her mail to the house but had obviously slipped up today.

'One came yesterday while I was out, and since I was late back I didn't come over with it last night,' he went on. 'The delivery of that one could have been a mistake. But when two more letters addressed to Lauren Frazer, The Lodge, Allardyce House came through the letterbox this morning, the mistake theory stopped being tenable.' He looked keenly down at her. 'She hired out your house, didn't she, that charming cousin of yours? And did it without so much as a word to you in advance. That's why you let yourself in to the place last Friday—and why you were so shocked when I told you I was renting it.'

Unable to deny his correct assumption, Lauren proceeded to attempt to make it seem as unimportant as possible.

'It's not my house in any real sense,' she said carelessly. 'It's like the rest of the Allardyce House property—it's used for business from time to time.'

'Pull the other one!' he said scornfully. 'If the place had been let out before, your cousin would have had a firm idea what rent to ask for it. And you would have found me in it and thought something like, "Oh bother! Donna's cocked it up again. Why can't that woman tell me what's going on?" Instead of which you were completely bowled over to be told that I was renting your home. You're not denying that it's your home, whether you own it or not?'

'I live there,' Lauren said uncomfortably, 'most of the time.'

'And you let me turn you out of your house without so much as a "Damn you!"'

Somehow they had stopped and were facing each other on the drive.

'What would have been the point?' Lauren said hotly. 'It was all cut and dried. Nothing I said was going to alter anything. It was so. . .so utterly humiliating.'

Unexpectedly he put up a hand and cupped her chin for a moment. 'Lauren Frazer, when are you going to begin to stand up for yourself?' His touch was warm and gentle. The unexpectedness of his gesture sent her feelings haywire. She forgot who he was, what she knew about him. She only knew that she felt hurt, and that he offered comfort. Her eyes were held by his, and she had the strongest urge to sink against that broad chest, let those strong yet so gentle arms hold her and keep the Donnas of the world at bay.

'I do believe,' he said softly, 'that if I did exactly what I am tempted to do at this very moment, you wouldn't so much as squeak in protest.' The desire in her intensified. She was drowning in those green eyes, hypnotised by them. . .and his arms, which had begun by steadying her, seemed to be drawing her towards him.

Suddenly what he had said penetrated her consciousness, bringing sanity in its wake. On a flood of shame she realised that she was on the point of being thrown completely off track by someone who had featured in a dish-the-dirt tabloid article—someone who was ready to take advantage of her vulnerability to make a pass at her. She dashed his hands away, hoping that she had hurt him as much as herself in doing so, and moved smartly backwards.

'No squeak necessary, Mr Lennox,' she said vehemently. 'Just be thankful I didn't bring my knee up.' She turned and strode blindly back towards the house, through the empty reception area and up to her room, carried on a wave of fury that was as much directed at herself as at the man she had left. What on earth had got into her back there? She sat on her bed, unable to find an answer.

There was a brisk tap and her bedroom door opened to reveal Charles Lennox, apparently not one whit abashed by what had happened on the drive.

'So this is where you've been put. I wouldn't exactly call it a fair exchange,' he said, taking a leisurely look round the room.

Lauren leapt to her feet. 'This floor is out of bounds to guests!'

'No prize for pointing that out.' His eyes surveyed the room in all its shabbiness. 'The Ritz it is not. These walls compare very badly with the highly professional job that's been made of the Lodge. *That* has quite obviously been given tender loving care by someone who has a feel for old places. This floor has been written off by someone who cares neither for places nor the people who have to live in them.'

Lauren leapt to her feet. 'Will you please get out of my room?'

He tossed her letters on to the bed. 'Don't get alarmed. I'm only returning the post you left scattered on the drive. Something must have upset you.' He actually smiled, but it was a taunting, infuriating smile. His eyes went slowly round the room again. 'Interesting to see just how far your cousin will go, and how far you are prepared to let her. To the end of the earth, it seems.'

'This is no business of yours,' Lauren said angrily. 'You have no right to intrude on my privacy.'

'But, my dear girl, haven't you been meekly letting me do just that, down at the Lodge?'

'Then isn't that enough for you? You have the whole of my house. Surely you can allow me the luxury of one room in what should be a private part of Allardyce House? From the moment you arrived you've been trying to interfere in my life!' she said passionately.

'Doesn't seem much of a life to me. What are you

waiting for? A knight in shining armour? Not many of those around these days. You might just have to do something about your own situation instead of waiting for a man to do the job for you.'

He closed the door and she stood staring at it, horrified. Was that how she came across to him? To everyone? Surely not. He was a devil who found pleasure in attempting to roast her in hell! She flung herself on the bed and pounded the mattress in sheer fury. She could kill the man! Slowly, painfully kill him.

She had actually meant to walk into the village for a local paper to check out the job front since she had this unexpected breathing space today, but now it was the last thing she could bring herself to do. It would seem too much like taking the abominable man's advice.

She gathered up a load of washing and went on to the staff kitchen to do it. It was a miracle that her clothes survived the furious pounding she gave them.

CHAPTER THREE

THE day Charles Lennox vacated the Lodge, Lauren was actually on her way back there when Donna waylaid her and asked her to come up to the flat for a quick word. Suspecting a request to spend either Saturday or Sunday working, Lauren followed her cousin warily, but found a glass of very good wine pressed into her hand.

'A drink to celebrate the weekend,' Donna said, so pleasantly that it was instantly alarming. 'Do sit down.'

'This is rather special,' Lauren ventured, raising her glass and sipping cautiously.

'Well, why not? I'm sure we've earned it.' Donna drank too, then looked studiously away from Lauren as she cleared her throat and said, 'Now, I've asked you to come up here because I'm afraid I need to talk to you about the Lodge. . .'

Lauren knew then. Her heart gave one violent thud of acknowledgement. The timing, the wine, the reference to the Lodge added up to a horrible total, and she felt the colour drain from her face as she listened.

'The past two weeks have been a bit of a revelation to me, I must say,' Donna went on, her tone confiding. 'I suppose I've been rather lazy about exploiting the full potential of this place. I'm like my mother. . .too soft-hearted to be a true businesswoman.' She gave a quick, empty smile in Lauren's direction. 'But I think we have to face up to reality and steel ourselves to make changes, Lauren. You know that business is not exactly booming. It would be crazy to turn down the chance of the sizeable rental it's possible to get for the Lodge. So—and this hurts me as much as it hurts you—I really can't see my way to letting you go back there, I'm afraid.'

'You can't mean that,' Lauren said, knowing that Donna did.

'Circumstances force me to mean it. I'm sorry.'

'But. . .Mum and I put hours of work into that house. Weeks and months and years of work.'

'And for every hour, week or month of work, you had years and years of rent-free accommodation.' Donna's tone might be gentle but her eyes had the steely look Lauren knew of old.

'Then let me pay rent for it now.'

'My dear Lauren, you couldn't begin to pay a market rent for the property. There's no future in thinking along those lines. I'm afraid there is nothing for you to do but accept that the past is just that, and come to terms with a new arrangement. I know it's a shock for you, but that's the way it has to be.'

Lauren felt absolutely pole-axed. All through the past week of being turned out of her home, it had never once occurred to her that the turning-out might be permanent. Perhaps she was a fool not to have foreseen this.

'I'd like to know exactly where I stand, Donna,' she said, forcing her cousin to meet her eyes. 'Are you getting round to telling me you want me to leave here altogether?'

There was a flicker of dismay on Donna's face.

'Lauren, darling! You don't think I would turn you out? Of course you'll go on living here. The top floor is virtually yours. When Maggie sleeps in it will feel like having a friend to stay.' She gave a conspiratorial smile. 'And I know you. Before long you'll be transforming the attics just as you transformed the Lodge.'

'Right now I can't think where I should get the time, the money or the energy to do that,' Lauren said with feeling. She put down her almost untouched drink, all appetite for it gone, and stood. 'Well, you've made the position crystal-clear. There's no point in talking any longer about it.'

'It's bound to take you a while to get used to the idea. I do understand how you feel. No desperate rush to move everything out. Any time in the next three or four days will do.' Donna drained her glass and helped herself to a refill, obviously not at all sorry to have the interview over.

Lauren drove down to the Lodge in a daze. The place was no longer her own. If she had to give it up, she was going to do it now. Already it had an alien feel as she wandered through it. The sitting-room was not her room with the desk Charles Lennox had used dominating it, his screwed-up papers in the waste-paper basket. In the bathroom were towels damp from his use, his discarded tablet of soap. She could even imagine the scent of his aftershave in the air. She flung open the windows, eager to remove all traces of his occupation as well as her own, wishing that the memory of his presence were as easy to eradicate.

It was habit that made her feel down the side of the sofa, a prime recovery-place for anything missing at the Lodge. The first item she pulled out brought a lump to her throat. It was one of the combs her mother used to wear in her hair. Lauren's eyes clouded with a million memories as she looked down at it, then she gave her shoulders an admonitory shake and tucked it determinedly in her pocket, resuming her search. No time for sadness over the past. The future held quite enough problems.

Her fingers encountered something hard. She worked the object out of the cramped space, and saw that she had found the missing pen which Charles Lennox valued so much, but not enough, apparently, to look in such an obvious place for it.

Charles Lennox, she thought furiously. He was at the root of it all. If he had not put the idea of renting out the Lodge into Donna's head, the present situation

would not have arisen. She would never forgive him.
Never!

She turned the slender gold barrel over in her fingers
and saw that there were words engraved on it.
'CHARLES—21.10.90'. Lauren's lip curled. A
memento of some perfect moment or other from an
appreciative girlfriend, no doubt. How kind of him to
retain fond memories of her—once he had got rid of
her, she supposed.

Half an hour later she was on her way to the address
he had left with her. She should have known better
than to expect Donna to deal with the matter. Donna
was busy getting ready for her bridge night, but
insisted that the pen should be returned at once to free
a valued client's memories of Allardyce House of all
suspicion. Lauren supposed she had a personal interest
in that, but she had an even bigger personal interest in
avoiding any further encounters with Charles Lennox.
This one would be a very brief encounter indeed if she
had anything to do with it.

His house, Longacre, was in a prime position at the
foot of the green and rounded Dassett Hills, its mellow
stone walls golden in the afternoon sun. Unfortunately
it appeared to be empty, and there were no approach-
ing footsteps when she knocked on the iron-studded
front door. Lauren walked round the back without
much hope. There was a row of stone outbuildings at
right-angles to the house with a flight of steps leading
up to a door on the first floor of the nearest building.
A woman was coming down these steps, shrugging on
a raincoat over a trim flowered overall.

Lauren told her she was looking for Charles Lennox,
but presumed he had not yet moved in.

'He's just moved into the service flat today.' She
pointed up the stone staircase. 'Not that you'll find
him there at the moment. He's somewhere in the
grounds. I'll give him a call. Who shall I say?'

'Lauren Frazer.' Lauren, fingers touching the pen in her pocket, waited, her eyes taking in the charming details of the place. There was a stone porch over the back door of the house, its lichened slate roof a roosting place for a pair of doves, snowy white against the fiery red of the Virginia creeper climbing the walls. A movement at the top of the service flat stairs caught Lauren's eye. A black cat with a white bib and paws came out of the high open door and sat looking down at her. She was trying with some difficulty to adjust to the idea of Charles Lennox as a cat person when he came through a stone archway at the end of the long velvety lawn.

He had lost no time in getting to work in the garden and was wearing a heavy fawn sweater and taupe cords tucked into green wellingtons. The latter were heavy with soil, and there was also a smudge of dirt across his forehead, which had an odd humanising effect, though the mocking smile with which he greeted her soon banished that.

'Missing me already?' he asked. 'Or did your curiosity get the better of you?'

'Neither!' Lauren said crisply. 'I'm here to return something you left behind, that's all. You left me your address for the specific purpose, if you remember.' She took the pen from her pocket and held it out to him.

'Good lord!' He took it, with a look of genuine pleasure transforming his face. 'I'd given up hope of ever seeing this again. Where was it?'

'Where I suggested it would be—in the Lodge. Down the back of the sofa, to be precise.'

'I checked there.' He was frowning.

'Not thoroughly enough. If you lose something while you are sitting on the cushions, there's a deeper gap for things to fall into.'

'There speaks the voice of experience.' He actually gave her a smile without undertones.

'Yes. We were always losing things down there.' Lauren thrust her hands deep in her pockets. Her fingers brushed against her mother's comb in her pocket and tightened around it. The feelings she had suppressed at the sight of it earlier in the afternoon welled up again and refused to be dealt with this time. It happened still from time to time, this upsurge of grief, but never had she been overtaken by it in more embarrassing circumstances.

'I'm very grateful,' Charles was saying. 'This pen was a present from my father to commemorate the move of my company to new London offices. He's dead now, and it was one of the last things he gave me, so I treasure it very much.'

Already struggling with her own emotions, Lauren found the warm feeling in his voice and the similarity of the circumstances he was speaking about and her own thoughts too much to cope with. She was mortified to feel a tear escape and begin to slide down her cheek.

He caught the quick movement of her hand as she tried to brush it away and looked up from the pen. 'Whatever is the matter?' he asked, his eyes studying her face, apparently concerned.

'Nothing. Absolutely nothing.' She turned, poised for flight.

He gripped her arm. 'Don't be so ridiculous. You're not going away in that state. Come up to the flat and have a drink or a cup of tea or something.'

'I don't want anything,' she said, swallowing hard and looking rebelliously at him.

'I don't suppose the impeccable Miss Frazer likes to be seen on the verge of tears, but you are, and I want to know why. This way.'

The brusque words sobered her as kindness would never have done. A firm hand under her elbow propelled her up the stone stairs to the service flat and installed her on the comfortable crimson settee in the sunny room. The black and white cat sauntered in, jumped up beside her and flopped against her thigh, purring. By the time Charles Lennox came through with coffee, Lauren's hand, taking the mug from him, was quite steady.

'Thanks. Sorry about that nonsense,' she said dismissively.

'What was it all about?'

Lauren had already decided that the quickest way out of the situation was to give him a truthful explanation.

'This,' she said, bringing the comb out of her pocket. 'And your reference to the pen being the last present your father had given you. I found the comb at the same time as the pen, and in the same place. It belonged to my mother. It's only a few weeks since she died. I don't give in to tears often, but they occasionally creep up on me. Sorry to have been such an embarrassment.'

'Something of an enigma, but not an embarrassment,' he said, adding unexpectedly, 'Sadness *is* unpredictable, as I know from personal experience. I'm sorry about your mother. The atmosphere of the home you shared indicates the kind of woman she must have been. In view of what you've just told me, I'm even more at a loss to understand how your cousin could behave so arbitrarily with your house. To say the charitable least, it shows a certain lack of finer feeling. I hope you're comfortably reinstated now?'

Lauren's creamy cheeks turned a dull pink and she avoided his eyes, gulping her coffee and referring to her watch. 'Goodness! Is that the time? I must go,' she said, getting hurriedly to her feet.

He stopped her completing the movement. 'Not so quickly. Does this mean you're not back in the Lodge?'

Lauren's eyes shone dangerously.

'No. Nor am I likely to go back now. If you must

know, Donna has been shown what a profitable business renting out the Lodge can be, and she intends to go on doing it.'

Not a flicker of discomfort showed on his alert face. Instead he returned her accusing look with a calm challenge.

'Then it's obvious, isn't it? You really are going to have to find yourself a better job.'

How easy it all was for him, with his wonderful old house and his business empire.

'With no qualifications? Not as easy to do as to suggest.'

'Get yourself some.' His reply was instant and brusque. 'Have a bit of initiative and arrange to sit the exams you missed. I take it that your mother's illness was the reason for your missing your finals? Surely the circumstances would predispose your college to allow you a second chance?'

'You speak from a privileged position,' Lauren said furiously, as full of anger now as she had been overwhelmed by sadness only moments ago. 'Let me tell you what life in the real world is like. If I leave the job at Allardyce House, I have no home. I'm unlikely to get a grant, having failed to complete my course first time around, and with the small amount of money I have in the bank I wouldn't last a term, let alone a year, if I had to support myself—nor would I have anywhere to live in college vacations. Life without a silver spoon must be hard for you to understand, Mr Lennox. And, not having been in the position of a dependent relative, you must also find it difficult to appreciate that, after being given a rent-free home for twenty-two years, I feel a certain obligation to my cousin and her family.'

'What I appreciate only too easily,' he said calmly, 'is that if you have no money in the bank after twenty-two years of rent-free accommodation, full-time work during those years by your mother, no doubt holiday

and weekend and evening work by you as soon as you
were old enough, then what your cousin's family lost
in rent, they more than made up for in economy where
salary was concerned. Be rational, Lauren Frazer. The
two of you have more than earned any favours your
family has done you. You're no fool. You must know
that. So there's got to be more than gratitude holding
you back. Are you sure you're not just a little bit
reluctant to come out from your safe grace-and-favour
accommodation and stand on your own two feet?'

'Please don't embark on that offensive line of accusation again.' Lauren tried to stand up, but the cat
anchored itself firmly to her thigh with razor-sharp
claws, making her gasp. 'Kindly remove your cat,' she
said tersely.

'Out of the way, Jeeves.' He scooped the animal
unceremoniously away from her and deposited it on
the floor. 'And now I suppose you're going to storm
off in high dudgeon again?'

'I'm leaving, yes. I'm in no mood for sermons.'

'Hoity-toity! Are you in the mood for this, then?'

She was given no time to guess his intention. She
found herself drawn towards him, his arms tightening
around her while he laughed down into her outraged
face. 'I think you need something to take your mind
off your troubles, Lauren Frazer. There's a whole
world of living and loving out there. Stop turning your
back on it. Get away from the doom and gloom and
take a chance on life.' He lowered his head and kissed
her protesting mouth against her fierce struggles at
first, then, as his hold tightened inexorably and the
demand of his mouth intensified, Lauren felt her will
to escape his unwanted embrace dissolving into an
overwhelming urge to mould her body to his. It was
all the more powerful because her mind was telling her
that this was the last kind of man she wanted to be
kissed by, while her humiliatingly submissive body was
taking not the least bit of notice. She wanted to let go

of reality, let herself float away on this blazing tide of feelings he was arousing in her. Oh, yes. . .she wanted. . .

Her body spoke for her, and he heard it. He gave a sleepy murmur against her lips, and his hands travelled the length of her spine in a slow, moulding caress.

Lauren surfaced with difficulty and snatched at her sanity. Sanity told her to thrust with all her strength against his chest and force herself away from him.

'How dare you? What do you think you're doing?' she protested ridiculously.

He laughed down at her, breathing hard. 'I was doing something I've felt like doing once or twice since I first met you. Don't try to tell me you had no taste for it yourself!'

'There was nothing to have a taste for,' she said vehemently, managing to release herself with one final thrust. 'It was a demonstration of what you consider to be your irresistible macho powers. You're a fool if you expect anyone to like that!'

He folded his arms and continued to look mockingly at her, unabashed. 'That wasn't the message I was getting just now.'

'I wasn't aware that you were into thinking of any reactions other than your own,' she said hotly.

'You can't talk yourself out of what happened. I kissed you because I fancied doing it. You resent it now, but you sure as hell responded to it. Believe me, I was fully aware of your reactions, but pretend if you want to. It was an enjoyable experience, but it was also a genuine attempt to prod you into tearing yourself away from your useless family and into a separate existence. I'd like to see you sorting out your life.'

She squared up to him, her diminutive figure challenging him with all the fury of David challenging Goliath. 'Why don't you sort your own life out? According to the papers, you have problems enough with that.'

She had got to him at last. His face became mask-like. 'I didn't have you down as a tabloid reader.'

'We have the full range of papers at Allardyce House. When a client features so prominently in one of them, we all read the article. It pays to be well informed about the people we deal with.'

His eyes were icy as they looked at her. 'And you believe every word you read? Every implication they care to make?'

'Are you suing them for damage to your reputation?'

'I wouldn't dream of letting them think they are sufficiently important.'

'Well, then.' Her tone and her look were pointed.

'Don't you think you are being just a touch naïve?' he asked. 'Any journalist's job is to take a perfectly reasonable happening and turn it into a story.'

'Not very difficult in your case.'

'So I'm earmarked as the Playboy of the Western World just because a trashy paper says so?'

'Nothing as dramatic as that,' Lauren said scathingly. 'Just someone not best placed to organise the lives of others. Perhaps now you'll damp down this personal interest in what happens to me.'

He raised his eyebrows in supercilious surprise. 'Oh, there's absolutely nothing personal about it. If I saw a road-sweeper whom I considered capable of doing something a little more challenging, I would be just as forthright with him.'

Lauren turned in the doorway, her eyes bright with the recurring urge to punch him on his interfering nose. 'And I imagine he would thank you for it as little as I do. Some people would define your attitude as a congenital inability to mind your own business.'

'And that would be their prerogative,' he said smoothly. 'Watch your step as you charge down the stairs—and thanks again for the pen.'

With the utmost difficulty Lauren negotiated the staircase. Every encounter with him left her with the desperate wish that she could rewrite the script and give herself better lines. She hadn't meant to bring up the newspaper article. Up to the point of reading about him, she had been contemptuous of tabloid overkill. But he hadn't really denied it, had he? Nor had his behaviour towards her. Her cheeks fired again, and her feelings sizzled as she made her way back to the place it no longer seemed suitable to call home.

It was not the best of times for Donna to accost her as she went back up the stairs, and inform her of a forgotten point—she was to show the estate agent round the Lodge on Monday, since she knew the place better than anyone and would make sure he saw it in its best light.

Suddenly, that was it, the final stab of the knife that convinced Lauren that the only sane course of action left was to head away from Allardyce House while there were still pleasant memories of the years there left.

Once the decision was made, it was as though a great weight was lifted from her mind. She turned round and went back down the stairs and out of the house again at once. She was going to head for the village and track down the Chelston local papers. Employers in this area would at least have heard of Allardyce House and the courses run there, so that might stand her in good stead. If Chelston didn't come up with something, then she would drive into Banbury and tackle the agencies there.

She had a sudden picture of Charles Lennox's lean self-assured face, looking smugly on at her decision.

Nothing to do with you, she told his ghostly presence in her mind with asperity. This is *my* decision, *my* move. But the thought that he would be pleased continued to hang around. So did the displeasure it engendered.

* * *

It was all accomplished with such surprising ease that Lauren found it difficult to believe her luck.

Holding out no more than slender hopes, one of the Banbury agencies sent her for interview with a training officer whose name Lauren happened to know since he had enrolled girls from his firm on the Allardyce House office management courses she had run. He had changed jobs and was now recruiting for Spencer Travis, who were about to open a branch in the area.

The management consultants' name was familiar to Lauren, having appeared frequently in headlines on the financial pages during her time at college. The rocketing success of Spencer Travis had often been referred to by lecturers as a prime example of the rewards of modern business methods.

She faced the interview with a mixture of philosophical calm and confidence, and talked for an hour and a half with Paul Bailey, whom she had always liked during her dealings with him, concealing nothing, but, as advised, emphasising her ability and experience.

Two days after the interview, the job offer came in the post. It was for a three months' trial, and she would have to work to gain her qualifications, but it was far more than Lauren had hoped.

Immediately she wrote with her acceptance, signed and returned the contract, and affirmed her willingness to do whatever was thought best to improve her status. Secretly she thought it flattering to have got the job through character rather than qualifications.

Telling Donna was unpleasant. Every possible accusation of ingratitude was made, and Donna became extremely hysterical. It was a relief in the end to drive away from Allardyce House.

Lauren had found a house to rent, the end house in Cherwell Terrace on the very edge of Banbury. It was dilapidated and Victorian, but it had possibilities. There were touches of dignity about its cornices and

elaborate plasterwork, and its rear windows overlooked open country with the River Cherwell only two
fields away. More important than all this, though: it
was Lauren's own place. It felt like a palace, even if
its glory was faded.

It was from this modest palace that Lauren emerged
before eight o'clock on her first day at Spencer Travis,
her eyes bright with the excitement of her new job.
She was wearing a new grey suit, a claret silk shirt,
and indecently expensive black shoes and handbag.
She had to keep telling herself that on her Spencer
Travis salary she could afford it all.

She had timed her arrival so that she would have
plenty of time to look around. She hung up her jacket
and ran an unnecessary comb through shiningly
immaculate hair, then wandered around while she
waited for Paul Bailey to arrive, touching the gleaming
wood surfaces of desks and cupboards with a proprie-
torial hand and wondering with a sense of eager
anticipation about the people who would be sitting at
the different work-stations.

She picked up a sheet of the firm's stationery from
the drawer of the desk that bore her name. The firm's
name was in fine gold italics, with the rest of the print
an elegant dove grey. It looked quietly distinguished.

It was then that her eyes went to the small print at
the bottom of the sheet. She read it perfunctorily, then
registered what she had read and went back for a
horrified second look. What she saw was there—she
had not been mistaken—suddenly extinguished the
glow of the day before it had even begun.

'Head Office, Knightsbridge, London SW1.
Managing Director—Charles Travis Lennox,' she
read.

Lauren swallowed convulsively. Not even the Travis
gave grounds for a saving hope that there could
actually be some other man with the same first and
family name. She remembered only too well the bold

signature on the cheques she had paid into the
Allardyce House account—C. T. Lennox.

It had to be him. At the head of the company giving
her the job she had been so proud to get was the last
man in the world she would choose to be working for.
And she was contracted to stay with the company for
three months at least.

'Oh, God!' she moaned. 'What have I done? And
worse—what on earth am I going to do?'

CHAPTER FOUR

ONCE the initial shock wore off, Lauren managed to rationalise the subject of the managing director. He would be in London most of the time, of course he would! The house in Oxfordshire was a weekend retreat. That was the way they all lived nowadays. With luck she would escape notice. She forced herself not to think of him.

Nothing in the first three weeks upset the imagined picture. She enjoyed the work enormously, and found Paul Bailey generous with praise and a real enthusiast for the job. Nothing untoward happened. She began to forget about the small print on the bottom of the official stationery.

Towards the end of the third week she was excited to be given her first chance to plan a training programme from scratch. On Friday afternoon she was lost in total concentration on the spread of papers before her.

She was vaguely conscious of someone walking into the office and going up to speak to Paul, but there was nothing unusual about that. In an open-plan office the knack of ignoring what didn't immediately concern you was quickly learned. It was when she raised her head in thought, not at first seeing anything but merely weighing two options, that she found herself looking across the heads of the workers in between into the unmistakable eyes of Charles Lennox.

He looked steadily back at her, not halting for a second in his conversation with Paul, while Lauren felt as though her circulation had stopped and wished she could shrink off the face of the earth. She bent over her work again, her concentration gone and her heart beating a tattoo in her chest.

Moments later a shadow fell on her desk and she was forced to look up.

'Well, well, well,' he said softly. 'I see you took my advice.' His eyes held hers. 'But I don't think I went so far as to suggest that you got a job in one of my own companies.'

Lauren answered as calmly as she could with those green eyes creating havoc in her, bringing the memory of their last encounter only too vividly back to her mind.

'I had no idea that this was your company, Mr Lennox. The name had no obvious connection with you, and it wasn't until my first day here that I realised you were the managing director. It was. . .quite a surprise.'

'I imagine so.' He injected a world of meaning into the three words. 'And one which I share. I think this is something we must discuss, don't you? Come up to my office in half an hour.'

Lauren had to dig the nails of one hand into the flesh of the other to stop herself trembling as he walked out of the office. He was going to throw her out, she was sure of it. She had been extremely rude to him at their last meeting, and he wouldn't want an employee with that sort of attitude and past experience of him.

'You've met Charles before, I take it?' Paul said, curiosity bringing him over to her desk.

'He used Allardyce House once a few weeks ago.' She tried to sound casual. 'Does he mean to spend much time here?'

'Oh, yes. He's got London running on oiled wheels now. I should think he'll spend the biggest part of the working week in Banbury until he feels that this branch is in the same happy state. Then presumably he will start up somewhere else. The man's a human dynamo.' Paul's voice was full of genuine admiration.

Lauren loaded paper into her typewriter when Paul went back to his desk. There was no point in waiting for the axe. She could see it falling already. And in any case, how could she work for a man whose reputation she knew, yet who continued to shake the foundations of her world like this every time she encountered him? Her fingers fumbled with the paper and she had to throw away the first two drafts of a resignation letter.

Charles Lennox's office on the top floor put paid to any idea that it was to be used as a temporary showplace. Bristling with computer and fax terminals, banks of filing cabinets and a battery of telephones, it was most definitely somewhere for real work to be done.

He rose briefly and indicated a chair. 'Sit down,' he said, his face for the moment inscrutable.

Lauren walked up to his desk and put the envelope she was holding on the teak surface in front of him. 'I don't think that will be necessary. I imagine my resignation is what you want.'

He took up the envelope, toying with it lightly while he spoke. 'And why should you think your resignation is called for?'

'It doesn't take much working out.'

'Aren't you forgetting something?' She looked doubtfully at him. 'I didn't appoint you. Paul did. I wouldn't dream of going over his head and accepting a resignation without discussing it with him first.'

'Then keep the letter until you've done so. Nothing about our last meeting makes me think you would find it acceptable to have me working in your company.'

He smiled in a way that made a shiver run down her spine. 'I can think of one or two moments that were not exactly unpleasant.'

She knew perfectly well which moments were in his mind, and his steady gaze was making the colour rise in her cheeks, forcing her to remember what she didn't at all want to remember.

'Then your recollection is very different from mine,' she said.

'I certainly recall the fact that you were prone to jump to conclusions then—just as you appear to have done today. Oh, for God's sake, sit down,' he said with sudden impatience. 'You wanted the job. Why the farce of pretending to throw it over now?'

'I'm not pretending. You were obviously unpleasantly surprised to find me here—just as I was to find you managing director.'

His gaze locked with hers. He rested his elbows on the desk, matching his fingertips precisely and looking over them. 'That brings us to the point, as far as I am concerned. Certainly I was surprised. But you're going to have to convince me that my appearance was as much of a shock to you.'

Lauren looked at him. What was he getting at? 'I told you it was,' she said.

'Well, you would, wouldn't you?' His steady stare was making her feel even worse than when she had come into his office.

'I really don't understand what you mean,' she told him.

'Then let me put it clearly. I'm not at all sure that this shock-horror reaction of yours isn't a put-up job.'

'Why would I bother to pretend?' Lauren was rapidly getting tired of his unreasonable prolonging of a painful business that ought to have been settled by now.

'Because it would be more diplomatic than letting it be known that you had deliberately moved to my firm in the expectation of getting preferential treatment.'

Her eyes widened and her cheeks went a fiery red as she stood up. 'Mr Lennox, my whole life has been lived out in an atmosphere of being done good to. I'm glad that particular phase is at an end. The last thing I want to do on leaving Allardyce House is to become anyone else's protégée. I hadn't the least idea that you had anything to do with this firm until the day I started here. Spencer Travis? It doesn't suggest you in the least.'

'My father's Christian names. I named the company after him.'

'I assure you nobody told me that.' She turned away. 'I'm not staying here to listen to more of your distasteful suspicions.'

'Oh—sit down!' He barked the words, and Lauren collapsed into the chair which was fortunately behind her. 'All right. Your outrage seems genuine enough. Now let's begin to talk sense.'

'Why should you think such a thing?' she said hotly.

'You're not here to question me. The reverse of that. How did you get the job? Did you know Bailey?'

She glared at him. 'Yes. But if you're implying what I think you're implying, I don't belong to the sleep-your-way-to-the-top brigade. Paul Bailey used Allardyce House courses. He liked what I did there. He knew my capabilities—my *working* capabilities. I got the job on the strength of what he knew I could do.'

He nodded. 'Fair enough. No need to blow your top. I could hardly be expected to believe you'd got it on the strength of your qualifications after what you told me. So. . .having been given the job, how are you getting on with it?'

'Paul has said that he's glad to have me on the staff.'

'That's not surprising. To say anything else would be to doubt his own judgement. I want to know how *you* feel about the work.'

'I like it very much,' she said reluctantly.

'Do better than that.'

'I've found it more challenging and interesting than anything I've done so far. Why are you making me say all this? Pure sadism?'

'I merely like to know what's going on in my own company. Sometimes I find out a little late in the day,' he added drily. He turned the envelope over and over in his fingers, his eyes resting broodingly on her. 'So now, having gone all out to get the job, and having admitted you enjoy it, you want me to believe that your resignation is serious, do you?'

'I think that shows you how I feel.' She nodded at the envelope. '"Circumstances alter cases. . ."' she quoted at him.

'I know—"Just as noses alter faces. . ."—and your pert little number is decidedly up in the air at the moment. Look—let's try to get things clear. *You* shot off whatever salvo is in this envelope because you flattered yourself that you knew exactly how *I* felt. Forget that. My thoughts are not as easy to read as either the tabloids or yourself seem to think. And yours, to put it mildly, seem a touch confused. Let me put a simple question to you. Do you feel yourself unable to work with me?'

'Work with you?' she echoed, unsure of where the question led.

'Exactly that. If I am to accept—and I've decided that I do—that you are here by accident, does working in a company you now know to be mine present problems? You were, to put it mildly, prickly enough in our encounters at Allardyce House. I put that down to your personal circumstances there. If I am wrong about that and there is a true personality conflict here, then it is as well for that fact to be recognised now.'

'Allardyce House was different,' she said slowly, unsure of her ground. He was confusing her. 'I did resent certain of your comments, because I felt that what went on there was to do with me, not an outsider. But this is your company, your world. Your opinions would automatically be expected and have prime importance.'

'A diplomat's answer! But if you mean it, it sounds

to me as though we can dispense with this.' He waved the envelope idly. 'What do you think?'

Lauren was silent for a moment. Then, 'How on earth do I know what I think?' she said in exasperation. 'You've made me go round in so many circles that I haven't a clear thought in my head.'

'Nonsense. You obviously want to keep the job.'

'What makes you so certain of that?' she asked.

'With no qualifications, you would hardly want to walk out of a first job you'd got more by luck than anything else with no references and a broken contract, would you?' Deliberately, he tore her envelope in two and dropped it in the bin, completely convinced by his own argument.

Lauren looked down at her hands, resenting his words but recognising their awful truth. She had made her high-flown gesture without really thinking about it. She raised her eyes to his. 'The decision appears to have been made.'

'And you appear to have an excellent opportunity to launch yourself on an interesting career. I presume you are not being such a fool as to turn it down.' For the first time he smiled, and her heart somersaulted, her defences threatened to crumble. He held out a hand across the desk. 'Shall we take it that the contract stands?'

She was undeniably relieved to have been stopped in her headlong rush out of a job she valued. But as his long fingers curved round her small hand, his touch brought instant recall of the more intimate contact of their last meeting, sending a hot stream of warning memory along her veins. She withdrew her hand hastily. His behaviour at Longacre was something that had to be dealt with if they were to work together, and there was no way of doing this by beating around the bush. He stood, and she followed suit.

'About what happened at Longacre. . .' she began tentatively.

'You prefer bargains to be sealed in that way?' His smile was taunting, but he had shown her that he knew very well what she meant.

'If you consider that sort of thing to be an unwritten clause in the contract,' she said, sticking firmly to her purpose, 'I must tell you that I'll be out of here quicker than a dose of salts.'

'Charmingly put. You'd leave for such a trivial reason?'

'I don't regard kisses as trivial, Mr Lennox,' she said, meeting his eyes directly. 'And I don't respect anyone who does so.'

The light of amusement in his eyes switched off. 'Don't worry. My personal life, as you have pointed out, is vigorous enough to engage me elsewhere.'

'Apart from that point of difference, I shall make every effort to make sure you have no cause to regret my appointment.'

'I don't go in for regrets,' he told her bluntly. 'You will either do your job well, or we shall part company at the end of your three months' probationary period. Could even be earlier than that. On Monday I shall be taking you to London with me to sit in on three different and very important training programmes we are running in the City. At the end of that we should both have a fair idea of whether this is going to work.'

It took all of Lauren's self-control not to show how much that floored her. He had thrown the assignment at her deliberately to catch her out, she knew.

'Whatever you say,' she said calmly. 'How long shall we be away?'

'Until the following Monday.'

'A week.' Her heart nose-dived even further at the thought of seven days in company she was sure she wouldn't find easy.

'All the details are here.' He handed her a typewritten sheet. 'I'll pick you up at six—a.m. not p.m. That's all, I think. I've delayed you long enough.'

When she reached the door, he said, 'And, Miss Frazer—I hope you manage to live up to your intentions. I don't fool easily.'

Paul read her face correctly as she went back into his office.

'He's told you about next week?'

'He has,' she said briefly, still reeling from the interview.

'Everyone does a familiarising stint in London. I was there for three weeks myself.' Paul grinned. 'But in any case, never expect plain sailing here. Life around Charles Lennox is full of surprises.'

And that, Lauren thought as she resumed work on the training scheme with half her mind on the week ahead, is something I'm already finding out.

'Got something pretty in here?' Charles Lennox asked, putting Lauren's case in the boot of the Lotus.

'Something suitable, I hope,' she said. 'I saw there was a social occasion listed for the end of the week.'

He gave her quick, disapproving look. 'You might sound as though you're prepared to enjoy it. Suitable, indeed!' He slung himself into the car's low seat. 'Perhaps it's the early hour.' He glanced at her house, which she had made sure he didn't set foot inside by being on the alert at her window. 'So this is your place. How does it compare with the Lodge?'

'Badly,' Lauren said honestly. 'But give me time. I'll lick it into shape. It has possibilities.'

'Like its owner.' He glanced down at her. 'It'll be interesting to see how you both turn out.'

He switched on the engine and the car leapt into life like a hungry tiger.

Already I can feel my hackles rising, Lauren thought. And it's not even five past six. The car ate up the miles through the misty morning and purred on to the motorway.

'How did that problematic cousin of yours take your

departure?' Charles Lennox asked, his long, elegant
fingers resting lightly on the wheel, his driving, like
everything else about him, totally assured. 'Did she
give you a hard time?'

'She wasn't best pleased.' She sensed his grin.

'I bet she wasn't. Have relations been broken off?'

'Temporarily suspended, I hope,' Lauren said. 'I
still have a certain fondness for Donna, in spite of all
that happened. I hope that we shan't lose touch
altogether.'

'I expect she'll find it politic not to do so.'

She glanced sidelong at him. 'That's a very cynical
attitude, Mr Lennox.'

'Realistic. And, by the way, I'm Charles to
colleagues.'

A wave of unease swept through Lauren at the step
towards familiarity. Her very existence was reason
enough to doubt the motives of over-friendly bosses.
She resolved to call him nothing at all.

'And now, Lauren, I suppose you'll avoid the use of
a name at all costs,' he said, infuriatingly hitting the
nail on the head.

'I think I can manage Charles when necessary,' she
said, her colour rising in contradiction. 'It's only one
syllable, after all.'

He laughed. 'Good!' He overtook a chain of cars
and settled into the inside lane again. 'Feeling
apprehensive?'

That depended on what he thought she might be
apprehensive about. 'I'm looking forward to seeing
more of the Spencer Travis empire. London too,' she
said. 'I've only been once—on an outing from school
to see the usual sights.'

'That's a sad state of affairs. We must see what we
can do to extend your knowledge this week.'

Did he imagine she was fishing for something like
that? Lauren said nothing. It seemed safer. After a
moment he said briskly, 'Now let's get down to talking

about work,' and launched into a clear, concise
account of the activities of Spencer Travis. Gradually
she relaxed, and as she put her own questions to him
her troublesome hackles subsided. The miles unrolled,
and it began to seem more possible that she and
Charles Lennox might manage to work together without too much hot air being generated. But as for the
closer relationship his switch to Christian names hinted
at, no. That was definitely not on.

Lauren kept strictly to her bargain during the week in
London. She was open, willing and friendly within the
bounds of the working day, but that was as far as it
went. It wasn't easy, because the more she saw of him,
the more attractive his company became, and she had
to remind herself forcefully both of his reputation and
her own reason to be wary of it. Several times Charles
suggested a drink or a drive before she went back to
her hotel, and once he offered her a meal at a London
nightspot where the Royals were often seen, and she
would have loved to take him up on that. She was
sorely tempted—and who wouldn't be?—but she kept
firmly to her resolve and politely thanked him as she
refused, pleading tiredness and the desire to be fresh
for work the next day.

'As you wish,' he'd said lightly when she turned
down the nightclub invitation. 'But talk of tiredness
cuts no ice with me. You still go along with the idea
that I'm a closet seducer, don't you?' And, shaking his
head with a mocking smile, he walked away without a
backward glance at her embarrassed face.

Whatever reservations she might have about Charles
Lennox in relation to herself, Lauren had developed a
sincere if grudging admiration for him as a business-
man and employer by the end of the week. She
watched him explain complicated matters to people
whose intelligence lacked the brilliance of his own, but
without any sign of patronage. She saw his total

mastery of any subject he was dealing with, and his firm, patient persistence until the people with whom he was working came close to the grasp of the subject he wished them to have. She saw him handle potentially difficult clients with dazzling skill, so that they were unaware of the manipulation they were undergoing and thought they had reached the decisions he wished them to make of their own accord. By the end of the week she was under no misapprehension that his success was due to luck. It came from hard work, consummate skill and outstanding talent. But he was still someone she had no intention of getting to know on a more personal basis.

Because she had declined all other offers, she was really looking forward to the one social occasion at the end of the week in which she could safely join. It was a theatre outing to mark the retirement because of ill health of one of the senior women on the London payroll. Tickets had been handed out, and a time fixed for meeting in the theatre foyer.

Lauren, her eyes glittering with excitement in anticipation of the fabulous musical to come, was there early. She was wearing a black dress by Monsoon which managed to blend innocence and sophistication in a highly satisfactory way, and over it a multi-coloured brocade jacket—a designer dress-shop bargain. Delicate, strappy sandals, dangling jet earrings and a pretty patent clutch-bag completed her outfit, and she was feeling good.

'Extremely suitable!' a voice said teasingly in her ear, instantly recalling for her the conversation they had had at the start of the week, and she turned to see Charles, debonair in dinner-jacket and bow tie, smiling at her. In spite of her proud words and noble resolution, her heart dissolved and her bones threatened to follow suit. He was so damned good-looking! Few men in the theatre crowd could hold a candle to him and he had the effect of making them all pale into insignificance. 'You look charming,' he went on. 'I am only sorry that I can't offer you a drink before we go in. As host I must wait here to greet everyone.'

Perversely, after having refused all previous invitations, Lauren found herself feeling regretful too, but she smiled brightly and said that she was about to go and look at the display of photographs of the stars in the foyer.

When she took her numbered seat in the theatre, on the front row of the dress circle, she found herself next to two empty seats. Last in came Charles and the retiring employee, Charles taking the place next to Lauren.

'Don't be alarmed. There's safety in numbers,' he said softly, smiling wickedly at her.

Lauren felt herself blushing. 'I would have thought that there were any number of people qualifying for the hot seat rather than a new employee,' she said.

'No doubt. But he who pays the piper calls the tune, and she who has refused to dance to it all week has to grin and bear it tonight.' Before she could think of a suitable reply, he turned and embarked on a conversation with his other neighbour which ended only when the lights dimmed and the orchestra began to play the overture.

The musical was every bit as good as reviews suggested, and Lauren was on a genuine high, her face radiant as she turned to Charles when the lights went up for the interval.

'Wasn't that wonderful?'

'I've been watching your face,' he said. 'Pity the cast can't. They'd find it extremely rewarding.'

Lauren felt suddenly exposed, much as one did in a dream of being naked in a public place. She managed to lose herself among the other guests during the interval drink in the private room reserved for them, and slipped back into her seat just as the lights were dimming for the second half.

The show had a rapturous reception, Lauren clapping until her hands tingled. She had been sufficiently taken out of herself to be able to turn and express her genuine thanks to Charles for the evening.

'You can say all that later,' he said, cutting her short. 'I'm giving you a lift back to the hotel.'

'Oh, that isn't necessary,' she said hurriedly.

'Perhaps not, but I intend doing it.'

'Marta is more in need of a lift.' The retiring member of staff was waiting for a hip replacement and walked with difficulty.

'Marta has got one.' His hand on her elbow was firm. Lauren looked over her shoulder, and saw that one of the other men was solicitously helping Marta down the stairs. 'Wait here. I'll bring the car round to the front. I'm parked at the side of the theatre.'

He disappeared. Lauren hesitated, frustrated by the feeling of being dragooned into something she didn't want. She frowned. Why should she meekly let it happen? She wasn't going to be browbeaten into a cosy ride back to the hotel with the possibility of unwanted developments to fend off. She stepped into the home-going crowds and hurried towards the Tube.

The London of the journey from the hotel to the theatre in waning daylight had been fine, but now, at a much later hour, the streets seemed to have changed character. Lauren felt conspicuous in her bright jacket and revealingly short skirt. People in the capital, she had noticed, seemed to avoid looking at each other in daylight, but now she was conscious of eyes taking in every detail of her appearance.

At the corner of the street, she was surrounded by a crowd of boys who had drunk too much and fancied a bit of fun with her. She ignored their taunts and catcalls and kept walking, but when they continued to go along with her, now dancing along in front of her, now on either side crowding in on her, she began to be afraid.

'Lauren!' The voice was the most welcome sound she had ever heard. A familiar car had stopped at the pavement edge, and Charles was coming round the bonnet towards her, with the boys melting away at the sight of him.

'On your way!' he told them, sounding almost bored, but looking incredibly tall and assured and fit. The last one left with a sheepish grin. Charles turned to her. 'Idiot! Get in,' he told her brusquely.

'I would have been all right,' she said feebly.

'Would you?' There was scepticism in his voice. He slammed the door on her and came round to the driving side, getting in without further comment.

'I left because I didn't think it necessary to take you out of your way,' she said into the silence.

'Really? I've been staying at Barker's all week.'

Her hotel. She looked at him in complete astonishment. 'I haven't seen you. I had no idea you were there.'

He gave her a withering look. 'Forgive me for being unaware that my movements had to be explained.'

'I thought you would have an apartment in town.'

'So I have. Friends on honeymoon are staying there this week.' Another look in her direction. 'Don't tell me. If you had known, you'd have run away from the hotel as you ran away from the theatre!'

He was making her feel thoroughly stupid. Perhaps he was justified in doing so.

He drew up in front of Barker's in the quiet square not ten minutes' walk away from the Spencer Travis offices, and came round to open the car door for her.

'A word of warning,' he told her coldly. 'Beware of fighting ghosts. It can make you miss the genuine real live enemy. And now run off to the nursery and get into your cot.'

Up in her room, Lauren tore off her clothes and lost no time removing her make-up, furious with herself and with Charles Lennox for underlining her stupidity.

But he had not yet finished with her. She was about to get into bed when there was a knock on her door and his deep voice said, 'You left your bag in the car. It's outside the door. Don't delay long enough to put on a suit of armour or someone else will walk off with it!' His footsteps faded away down the corridor and, when Lauren cautiously opened the door, there was no one in sight.

She felt more ridiculous than ever. All week he had been under the same roof, and not one unwelcome move had he made. It gave a Victorian melodrama feel to her own behaviour. She dived back into bed and, until she went to sleep, spent some time rewriting the scenario of the day to cast a more sensible light on herself, wishing she could do the same thing to Charles Lennox's memory.

On the drive back they talked business but Lauren was conscious all the time of the previous night's fiasco. When they reached her little house, she swallowed hard and said, 'Thank you for the lift, and again for the wonderful show last night. Can I offer you a cup of coffee?' It was what she would have said to anyone else. Why not to him? So why was her heart pounding so wildly?

He had gone round to the boot for her case, and as he put it down on the step his green, amused eyes looked down at her.

'Thanks for the honour, but I have things to do at home, so you can relax.'

He knew exactly how she was feeling. Lauren, for the umpteenth time since she had met him, blushed. 'That's fine. I don't want to delay you,' she said.

'You won't,' he told her suavely. 'Try not to hold it against me. I hope you've learned a satisfactory amount this week. Here's one final lesson for you: think too hard about what you fear may happen, and you'll will it into existence.' He bent so swiftly that she

closed her eyes in reflex, then the unhurried caress of
his lips on hers sent reaction quivering through her.
'And that, my suspicious little Lauren, is no more than
you deserve on this particular occasion,' he said softly.

Then he was back in the car again, starting up the
engine and roaring off along the terrace while his
mocking laughter rang in her ears.

Seized by childish temper, Lauren kicked a stone
after the car. A couple of toots on the horn proved
that he had seen her do so.

'Oh, damn you!' she muttered savagely as she let
herself into the house. 'I was right all along. That's the
last attempt at a friendly gesture I'll be fool enough
to make.'

CHAPTER FIVE

THROUGH plate-glass windows the rounded green hills and river valleys of the Derbyshire Peak District formed a backdrop for Charles Lennox as he stood, lost in concentration at the front of the group, looking down at the papers on the table. At present the room was quiet while the students read through duplicated sheets of his observations from the morning session prior to discussion.

Lauren's job was to note not only comments but personal reactions and body language as the group discussed the rights and wrongs of the way they had been running their business. At the moment, however, she found herself covertly watching Charles, not the students, and doodling idly on her notepad. He looked up briefly, but not at her. How well she was beginning to read the changes in those green eyes of his. She knew all their variations, from the fir-green of displeasure to the dappled sea-green of amusement. Almost all their variations. . .

Her own eyes went cloudy with thought. She found herself wondering how the green eyes changed when he was making love. The lead of her pencil snapped and he looked quickly up at her. Both pencil and pad slipped out of her grasp and she was glad of the opportunity to dive out of sight. When she straightened up cautiously, Charles was about to start work. Just as well, Lauren thought, scarcely able to believe the track her daydreaming had followed. She never used to have thoughts like these. Sometimes she hardly knew herself nowadays.

She had worked with Charles several times since the session in London, but this weekend stint in

Derbyshire was the first time an overnight stay had been called for since London and there was no denying that she was nervous about it.

She had kept to her resolve not to become one degree more involved with him on a personal level, and her ultra-correct attitude had at first seemed to amuse him, but latterly his reaction had been more difficult to assess. At times she felt that he was becoming impatient with her, but she didn't know what to do to defuse the tension between them. She found him far too attractive and potentially dangerous to relax with him.

Charles began speaking, and gradually the course content took precedence over its leader until work ended at five. Charles seemed preoccupied, and Lauren had to remind him that she hadn't got the names and agenda for the Sunday course.

He stretched, easing away the tension of the day.

'No hurry. We'll talk about tomorrow over dinner.'

'Isn't that cutting it a bit fine?'

He gave her the fir-green look. 'This evening, I said, Lauren. Right now, I want a shower, a change of clothes, and no talking.'

Lauren walked briskly round the conference centre grounds, then went up to her room, ran a bath, and took her time over it. The solitary dinner with Charles loomed large. She helped herself to Dutch courage in the shape of a vodka and tonic from her personal bar, then read a while until it was time to put on her war-paint.

The 'dressy' frock she had brought with her had seemed decorous enough when she packed it. It was a fine coffee-coloured jersey with a high roll neck and long sleeves, newly bought. When she slipped it on, though, it was quite obviously not at all as modest as it had seemed in the shop. It *clung*, though rather flatteringly. The skirt swirled with soft seduction when she turned, and the dress as a whole managed at the same time both to cover and to reveal the body beneath it. Lauren clasped a couple of long gold chains round her neck, then agonised over whether they drew attention from or towards an area the dress was already doing quite enough to promote.

Something Charles Lennox had said came into her mind. Why did she so frequently remember his words? Now she was doing exactly what he had warned her against—risking making something happen by dwelling on it. It any case, it was time she went down to the dining-room. She left the chains in place. If Charles Lennox uttered the tiniest smooth compliment, she would strangle him with them. With a last desperate glance at the mirror she headed for the stairs.

Charles rose, smiling, as she walked across the bar towards him. He looked refreshed and elegant in a superbly tailored taupe suit. Lauren thought that what she felt at the sight of him must be like the attraction of a magnetic pole. Had her mother struggled against something like this? Struggled and given in? *She* was not going to give in, not in a million years.

'What will you have? Your usual vodka and tonic?' he asked.

How dared he assume that he knew her preference? 'A Perrier, thanks,' she said, adding, when he gave her a questioning glance, 'with ice and lemon.'

'Like that, is it?' he said. 'I shall take care not to consult you about the wine list.'

The arrival of the wine waiter saved Lauren the need to answer that, and selection of the meal and an analysis of the day's courses took them safely up to the arrival of the first course at their window table in the dining-room.

'You said we would talk about tomorrow,' Lauren said, cutting delicately into her quail tartlet.

'Yes, by all means.' He waited until she looked expectantly at him, then asked, 'What would you like to do?'

Lauren's knife and fork poised motionless in mid-air. 'What do you mean?'

'Just that. Name your preference, and I'll organise it.'

She slowly lowered her knife and fork. 'I was under the impression that we were running a course here tomorrow.'

'That's what I meant you to think. But that isn't so. I thought we needed a day to sort things out between us.'

'I don't believe this!' she said with furious emphasis. 'Are you telling me that there's nothing scheduled for tomorrow?'

'On the contrary. The day is earmarked for the express purpose I've just spelled out. Don't look so exceedingly bad-tempered.'

'How do you expect me to look when you book me in here tonight for a next-day course that just isn't happening?'

'I knew that if I put the need for a talk to you openly, you'd run a mile. Finish your tartlet. It looks too good to waste. And listen to what I have to say.'

He watched her steadily until she swallowed down her anger and with the utmost difficulty resumed eating the food which now tasted like sawdust in her mouth. Only then did he carry on speaking.

'At the start, I thought you could only mean trouble. I tried to sort it out and thought I had succeeded. But the invisible barrier is still there. It prevents the free exchange of ideas. It stops the development of a proper working relationship. What is it with you, Lauren? I need to know why you are so afraid of me.'

'I'm afraid of no one.' She flashed a furious glance at him.

'Wary, then. Perpetually on guard. Why is that?'

'You ask that after what you've done?'

He looked scornfully into her accusing brown eyes. 'Come off it, Lauren. We've stayed in the same hotel before, and I assure you that if I fancied spending a night with a girl it wouldn't be with one who wanted to drown the whole proceedings in ice and lemon! There'd have to be as much warm, full-blooded enjoyment on her part as there would be on mine. All I want to do is get to the bottom of what's bugging you and ruining our working relationship. Business premises with constant interruptions are hardly the place for sorting out that kind of problem.'

'Very noble. If your motives were otherwise, I don't suppose you'd openly admit it,' she said stiffly.

'You have a real hang-up about getting involved with your boss, don't you? he said, looking keenly at her. 'Why don't you tell me what happened, and see if that clears the air?'

'Nothing happened to me!' she said vehemently.

She could see him thinking hard. And thinking along the right lines. 'Then if not you, your mother. Is that what it is? Does no mention of a father and the need for family charity add up to a problem of that kind? Was she the wrong sort of act to follow?'

The waiter came up to the table and removed the first course plates. Another approached and conjured with cutlery, then there was a lull which allowed Lauren to ask, her voice tight with anger, 'Don't you think you are making an unwarranted intrusion into my private life?'

'I don't call it an intrusion. If your private life cripples your working one, then it becomes my business.'

The waiter hovered again, bringing their main course, offering vegetables, oblivious of the heavy atmosphere at the table.

'So how about humouring me?' Charles said calmly when the man had disappeared again.

'I don't humour voyeuristic curiosity.' Lauren attacked her salmon as though she were sinking her knife into his flesh.

'Neither of those things. Interest—and for a definite reason. Don't try to kill that poor salmon. It's dead already.'

'For two pins I'd get up and go this instant.'

'But you won't.' His eyes were a clear, intense green as they rested on her. 'Because you know that I have no intention of letting you bolt for shelter this time.'

'I shall not stay here tonight,' she burst out with stifled fury.

'You'll find it hard to get away. The last train's gone. There might be a bus, but there's such a chain of them to link up between here and Banbury that by the time you got to the third one they'd all be back in the depot for the night.'

'Then I'll ring for a taxi to take me home. And I don't care if it costs me a month's salary.'

'Believe me, you will stay.' There was pure steel in his voice. 'You had two free days during the week to allow for a working weekend. Tomorrow is legally mine, like it or not.'

'A day's work is yours, perhaps, but not a day's socialising.'

'If you insist on working, I can find work for you to do. But it won't stop me talking and making you talk. I think it would be far more pleasant to enjoy a day out—and any normal person would have difficulty in finding anything wrong in that.'

The waiter approached after another heavy silence.

'We'll have two portions of *tarte aux fraises*,' Charles said, not even giving Lauren the choice, 'and coffee at the same time, after which we prefer not to be disturbed.'

'I never eat high-calorie desserts,' Lauren said stonily.

'Tonight I think you'll find that you can. Anger burns an amazing number of calories.'

She had meant to take a mouthful or two, but it was

so good that the rest of the *tarte* disappeared as though by magic.

'What did I tell you?' Charles said with satisfaction, pushing his plate aside and reaching for the coffee. 'Black or white?'

'Black, please.' The fight seemed to be going out of her. Perhaps he sensed it, for he suddenly reached across the table and put his hand over hers.

'Come on, Lauren,' he said softly. 'Talk to me.'

She looked at his hand on hers, at the pattern of his skin, the dark hair on his wrist, the shape of his nails. There was something achingly comforting about his touch, but at the same time it sent danger signals through her veins to speed up her heartbeat, alarm her mind. She drew her hand away from the pressure of his.

'It was a rotten trick to get me here on false pretences.'

'How else would I have ensured that you'd stick around long enough to shed any light on this no-go area of yours?'

'It'll always be there. I don't mix work and pleasure.'

'But if I understand why, then we can both accept it and get on with the business of working together—I hope with considerably less tension than there is at present.'

Slowly she raised her eyes and looked at him. Genuine, or dangerous? He was watching her with such an open, questioning look that suddenly—though she was still smarting at the way he was relentlessly forcing her into it—she did want to talk to him. After a lifetime of pretending that her father had died when she was a baby, to be confronted by someone who was neither taken in by the pretence nor politely going along with it was rather like the possibility of having the poison in a wound drained.

She took a long, considering drink of coffee.

'All right. I'll talk,' she said.

He put his own cup down. The green eyes looked approvingly at her. 'Good.' He leaned back in his chair. 'I'm listening.'

She concentrated on the delicate silver coffee-spoon that she had picked out of the saucer and was fiddling with. 'You are right, of course, in assuming that what happened to my mother has coloured my attitude. My father, as the blank space on my birth certificate suggests, had no desire whatsoever for the relationship, and even less for public acknowledgement of it. I can't expect you to understand how hurtful that blank space is—that total void—a half-denial of my existence. My mother must have been the greatest of innocents when she began working for him. He went for gratitude at first—drove her home if she was working late, helped her with problems with her landlord—who better than a solicitor to do that? He confided in her about his unhappy marriage as time went on. It seemed so sad, she thought, that a kind man like him should be so unhappy. Eventually, long after she had fallen hopelessly in love with him, he disposed of her scruples, one by one. He loved her too. Why should it be wrong for them to snatch what happiness they could? There was no reason for her to feel guilty when his marriage had already irretrievably broken down. When the time was right, he would divorce his uncaring wife. Not now, because she was ill. Not months later, because his son was too young yet to cope with the trauma. And so it went on. The old, old story of the man who never will, and the girl who can't give up hoping that he might. It could have gone on much longer if the shock of my impending arrival on the scene hadn't well and truly brought his real self to the surface so that even my innocent, trusting mother could see him for the shallow character he was.'

The fragile spoon bent suddenly under the pressure

of Lauren's fingers. Charles took it from her and straightened it, then put it back in her saucer.

'Sorry,' she said briefly. 'I haven't spoken about this to anyone before. Now I know why. It affects me more than I thought.'

'Understandably.' She was glad of his matter-of-factness, his avoidance of sickly sympathy. 'Go on when you're ready.'

'The rest is pretty obvious. My mother's lapse—because of course he blamed her entirely for the pregnancy—was to be got rid of. No other option could be considered. But to my mother I was an object of love, not something to be disposed of as an inconvenience. He offered her money to go away—a long way away. She agreed to go, indeed wanted to go, she was so devastated by his attitude—but she refused his money. She never communicated with him or heard from him again. But do you know, when she saw his death announcement in the *Telegraph* she actually cried for him. She'd told me about him when I was fourteen, and I was nineteen when he died. I found her tears incomprehensible, but the moral of her story plain. Never get too closely involved with an employer. That way danger lies.'

Charles was silent for a moment, then he asked quietly, 'Isn't it rather cynical to lump all employers in the same category?'

'It might be cynical, but at least it's safe.'

'Not just the least little bit offensive?'

She met his eyes steadily. 'On a personal level, I have to say that nothing I have learned about you has changed my mind.'

A worldly-wise expression crossed his face. 'My all too public reputation!'

'Which you haven't denied.'

'Which I haven't explained.'

'I'm not the one asking for explanations. You are.'

'Did you ever try to see your father?' That particular

question led to an area she was incapable of discussing with anyone. She was thankful for the way he had framed it, which made it easy for her to deceive him.

'No. I never tried to see him.'

'You don't think he might have had second thoughts?'

'Even my mother, besotted though she was, didn't think that.'

There was silence between them for a while. Eventually Charles said, 'Thank you for speaking so honestly. It explains a lot.' His tone changed. 'Now—what would you like to do tomorrow?'

Lauren looked at him with astonished disbelief. 'Haven't I just been telling you why I don't want days like tomorrow?'

'On the contrary. You've been telling me why you don't want days completely *unlike* tomorrow. All I had in mind was a walk along Dovedale, lunch somewhere agreeable, and perhaps a visit to Chatsworth House before the run home. Since all three places are extremely public on an Indian summer weekend like this one, I hardly think the proposal holds any danger. And be rational—haven't I publicly proved my desire not to be involved with any woman? You saw it in the paper.'

He was making her laugh with him.

'You're an impossible man,' she said.

'So I've been told.'

'I just don't know what you expect to achieve by it.'

He looked into her eyes, his own lively with challenge.

'A cooling-down, easing-off time. And afterwards, better collaboration. Nothing more sinister than that.'

Perhaps she *was* over-reacting, both to the past and the present. In all the weeks she had been working in his company he certainly hadn't done anything that could be interpreted as making a pass. Perhaps his wanting to understand her attitude was justified in his eyes. He spent his whole life questioning motives and purposes in the business field, after all. She took refuge behind her coffee-cup and sipped slowly, thinking.

The day out he proposed attracted her. She had spent all her weekends since leaving Allardyce House skivvying away at Cherwell Terrace, and all the rest of the week working her socks off. It would be lovely to do something a little frivolous for once.

She put down her cup. 'Oh, what the hell! All right, then,' she told him. 'I could do with a day in the fresh air.'

He grinned approvingly. 'Good for you. That nose is far too nice to be cut off!'

It was a mistake. Lauren had known in her heart of hearts that it would be.

At first it was the harmless, golden October day she had hoped for. The waters of the Dove beside which they walked danced with light, and the sun gilded the strange shapes of the limestone rocks—Dovedale Castle and Lovers' Leap and the slender columns of Tissington Spires. Charles named them all for her, and at the other end of the scale showed her the smallest flora of the area, miniature treasures she would have missed if he hadn't pointed them out.

But then he took her off on a short detour to see Reynard's Cave, and that was the turning point in the day.

Once inside the forty-foot arch of the entrance, the interior of the cave was shadowy and mysterious, with the musty smell of secret places. Lauren glanced at Charles, suddenly aware that they were alone and that none of the other riverside walkers had made the detour. He was looking up, his hands on his hips, his stance easy and relaxed. But Lauren didn't feel relaxed. His hair had been blown by the breeze into rugged, attractive disorder. She very much wanted to touch it, and the urge was so strong that she had to do something to break its power.

She cupped her hands to her mouth and called a sudden 'halloo-o-o' to awaken the echo she was sure there would be and create the illusion that they were not alone. Instead she was rewarded by the sudden clatter and swoop of what seemed like hundreds of bats, as startled as she was.

The instinctive reaction that made her fling herself against Charles in her fright, hiding her face against him, her arms flying up to protect her head until the frenzied air became less violently disturbed was wholly innocent.

'Have they settled?' she asked fearfully, her voice muffled.

'Almost.' She could feel his voice as well as hear it. 'Keep still. A few are still swooping around.' A comforting arm came round her.

And there the innocence stopped. As panic receded, she found herself clinging to him for the sheer sensuality of it, her face pressed against his warm chest. She heard his heart beating, breathed in the clean, fresh scent of his skin through the fine cotton of his sweater, melted in the strength of his arm. Her physical pleasure increased headily as the air grew still around them. Still, and yet alive with a vibrant expectation.

She felt his hand on her face. 'Hey!' he said softly. 'You're all right, you know. . . Nothing's going to hurt you.'

Then she did the maddest thing of all. She turned her face into his hand, pressing her mouth into the soft warmth of his palm against her lips.

Realisation of what she was doing erupted like a storm in her. She pulled away from him, the dark power of her own feelings creating a panic far greater than anything engendered by the dark shapes now clustered in the recesses of the cave. But his arm

tightened around her and though she avoided looking
at him she could sense that he was looking hard at her.

'Not liking bats isn't a capital offence,' he said
gently. 'Take your time.' He hadn't noticed? His next
words robbed her of that faint hope. There was
humour in his voice. 'I'm not objecting. It makes quite
a change from your normal attitude.'

She went hot then cold with shame. 'Let's get out of
here,' she said brusquely, tugging away from him and
heading for the mouth of the cave.

He strolled easily at her side, looking down at her.
'And now I suppose you're going to punish both of us
for an entirely natural reaction.' The green eyes glit-
tered. 'To the bats. . .' he added, then gave a full-
throated laugh. 'Oh, that wasn't fair. No way am I in
danger of mistaking panic for passion. I've got a flask
in my haversack. I think we need a coffee.'

Lauren needed time to recover, and wandered off
with her plastic cup down to the river's edge where she
stood staring into the clear waters of the Dove where
brown trout basked, seeing nothing.

Was she as vulnerable as her mother? she wondered,
brooding on the incident in the cave. If anyone had
put that to her as a possible scenario, she would have
sworn she would prefer to suffer any kind of alarm
than to cling to the very man she had been intent on
distancing. And yet it seemed so instinctively natural. . .until she had got her mind back into gear again.

She brooded on, profoundly shocked by what had
happened. Eventually Charles joined her.

'Time's getting on. Shall we make a move? I don't
think we'll manage to fit Chatsworth in. By the time
we've had a good, leisurely lunch, the afternoon will
have gone.'

'I don't want to be late back. I've a lot to do at
home,' she told him dismissively.

'We'll put the visit on hold for another day.'

She looked coolly at him. 'We don't have another day. I only owe you this one.'

He took her empty cup and rinsed it in the river, then stowed it with his in the knapsack. His green eyes looked challengingly into hers. 'We'd better make the most of it, then, hadn't we, if you're to strike such a hard bargain?' he said.

They resumed walking, with Lauren resolved to be on her guard, but the sun and the river and the beautiful countryside combined with the security given by other walkers to lull her into enjoyment once more, and lunch at a delightful Elizabethan manor house-turned-restaurant went on until late in the afternoon.

Looking back on the day when she was home once again, Lauren forced herself to be honest and admitted soberly to herself that Charles Lennox was worming his way into her approval. She had somehow during the sunlit hours managed to forget the devious way he had planned for them to spend time together. He had behaved impeccably, and yet somehow by the end of the day she knew that she had crossed the barrier she wanted to keep between them.

He was too clever by half. Too good at getting his own way, too good at disarming opposition, too good at organising everything and everybody. But she was not going to become a victim of his subtle management skills.

Today had happened. Nothing could undo it. But it was a one-off. There would be no more like it. Not in a million years.

CHAPTER SIX

THE Indian summer ended, and the sudden change for the worse in the weather gave birth to an epidemic of influenza which caused headaches for Spencer Travis as well as for the scores of sufferers.

Lauren filled in on several occasions for her counterpart in the London office, and ran a couple of the less complicated courses without assistance. Paul was equally busy, and Charles was continually rushing up and down the country making sure that wheels turned smoothly in the difficult circumstances. She saw little of him, and gradually regained her confidence.

At the end of the second week Lauren was working late after everyone had gone, bringing her conference notes up to date. She had not known that Charles was in Banbury that day, and was surprised when he put his head round her door at that late hour.

'Thank goodness you're here,' he said with feeling. 'Are you well? I hope to God you are because I'm going to ask a favour.'

'You mean you're not just concerned for my welfare?' she said ironically, thinking that he looked as whacked as she felt, and no wonder, for they had all been working like slaves.

'I need an assessment prepared for the firm I'm seeing on Monday—like we used in Derbyshire, remember? My secretary's off ill and the girl from the pool who stayed behind to do it has collapsed on me. I've just taken her home. Could I ask you to do the work over the weekend? There's no one else I can get hold of without more hassle, and I've shoals of reading to do myself for a new client I'm meeting tomorrow.'

He scanned her face. 'Several hours' work. I can imagine how little you need that.'

Lauren said goodbye to her plans for a restful couple of days. He had driven up and down the motorway more times than she could bear to think, and it didn't sound as though there was any respite this weekend for him, either.

'No problem,' she said simply. She looked at the sheaf of papers in his hand. 'Is that it?'

'Most of it, apart from the section I was working on last night, which is at Longacre, I've realised. If I can give you a lift home, I'll pop back with the missing bit when I've dropped you off.'

'No need for a lift, thanks. I've got my car. Any time to suit you will do. I've no other plans for tonight.'

His look was full of gratitude. 'I know what your schedule has been like. Thanks, Lauren. I'll see you later.'

'Fine. May I take a typewriter? Mine misses bits of letters.'

'I'll bring one. You see to the stationery you need.'

He disappeared at once, and Lauren, after getting together all she required, abandoned thoughts of shopping and headed home.

It was nine o'clock when she put down her after-dinner coffee and opened the door to Charles.

'Come in,' she said, taking the typewriter from him and putting it down on the floor. 'Goodness!' she added as he stepped into the light and she saw the state of him. 'You're wet through. What on earth have you been doing?' There was also a smudge on his face which she was too polite to mention.

'Changing a wheel for a kid who must have only just passed her test. Why do such incidents always crop up when it's pouring down?' He was carefully shrugging himself out of his dripping Barbour jacket. 'What can I do with this?'

'I'll put it in the kitchen. Help yourself to coffee if you'd like some. I won't be a minute.'

When she came back he was standing in front of the glowing coal fire, one cup of coffee already dispatched.

'That's better,' he said thankfully.

She refilled his cup. 'Have you eaten? I—I could rustle something up if necessary.'

'There's food at home when I have time to eat it. I'll just go through this lot with you as quickly as possible.'

He looked so utterly exhausted. She had thought that the busy two weeks had helped her regain distance between them, but suddenly she found herself wanting to pull his dark head down on to her shoulder, to cradle him in her arms and tell him to rest.

He drew a chair up to the table and looked up at her.

'Ready when you are.'

Lauren sat down, searingly conscious of the length of his thigh brushing against hers and the movement of his arm against her own as he turned over the papers on the table. He had showered and changed before coming back. She could smell the faint, distinctive scent of sandalwood, and, when he roughly brushed back his hair, she recognised the shampoo he had used. Why were her senses suddenly so super-aware, her muscles tensing at the slightest movement? She focused on the work in front of her, forcing herself with difficulty to think of it, and nothing else.

'Can you make sense of it? he asked finally.

'I'm sure I can.'

'Thanks, Lauren. I'm grateful.'

She looked up at him and was instantly disconcerted to meet his eyes at such close quarters. 'You don't have to be,' she said awkwardly, striving for normality. 'It's my job.'

'An extended version of it, piling all this on you.'

She shrugged. 'We're all working hard—you as much as anyone.'

'So I should. It's my business.'

'I've known a boss with quite different ideas.'

He smiled. 'I remember. But that's all over now.'

He looked round her room, the only she had succeeded so far in bringing up to an attractive standard of furnishing and decoration. The light from lamps and flickering fire fell on soft peach walls, almond green carpet, and pastel loose covers and curtains. Antique pieces from the Lodge looked very much at home.

'What a pleasant place this is,' he said. 'You have a definite gift for interior decorating.'

'Thanks to Donna. It wasn't her strong point. She left that kind of thing to me. I enjoyed it.'

'That shows—as it did in your old home. I hadn't realised that the décor at Allardyce House was your work too. You could have made a career in that field. Did you never consider it?'

'You need capital for that kind of business.'

'Capital can be arranged if the client looks good.'

Lauren pushed back her chair, beginning to get the familiar feeling of being taken in hand and moulded. 'Look, Charles, let's skip the career fantasising for tonight. I'm far too bushed. . .'

He stood too. 'The habit dies hard.' He looked down at her thoughtfully, then appeared to make up his mind about something. 'If fantasy doesn't appeal, let me tell you about a real work prospect that might help you through this weekend. I'm sending you out to the Grenada conference with Paul. You'll have to work hard again, but there should also be a bit of welcome relaxation, and I imagine that right now you feel as though you could do with that.'

'You're sending me? To the Caribbean?' Lauren said incredulously. 'I thought Marian from the London office was going.'

'So she was. But she's been out of action with flu for ten days, and she's a bit of an asthmatic. It's wiser for her to stay here. I'll let you have all the details. Pleased?'

'Delighted!' Lauren's dark eyes shone, and thoughts of the Caribbean were making her tiredness magically disappear.

'You look it.' He looked as though he was going to say more, but changed his mind. 'I'll get my coat before I fall asleep on my feet. Through here, wasn't it?'

'Let me.' Lauren darted in front of him to the kitchen, not wanting him to see that particular room. But he followed her in, and when she turned with his Barbour he was staring around.

The units, such as they were, looked as though they had come out of the ark and were a total hotchpotch of mismatched items painted a miserable brown. The sink was an original shallow stone affair with a wooden draining-board. Nothing but a complete refit could make the place acceptable.

'You shouldn't be living in a hole like this!' he exclaimed.

'The old couple who moved out had been here all their married lives. They obviously hadn't bothered the landlord to do much.'

'You're renting?' The idea obviously displeased him.

Lauren gave him a stony look. 'That's what ordinary people do, you know. Buying houses takes money. Lots of it.'

'You realise that replacing these antiquities means that whatever you replace them with belongs to the landlord, who will no doubt be grateful for your sacrifice and promptly put the rent up?'

'Of course I know that,' she said impatiently. 'But I don't intend to live with this mess for any longer than I can help. It will be ages before I can begin to think of buying a house.'

'Why on earth didn't you talk to me about it? You

could have a company loan for the full amount. You can still have one.'

He was doing it again, getting a grip on her life and twisting it into the shape he thought it should be. Lauren's face was set.

'Thank you, but that won't be necessary. Here's your coat.'

Exhaustion meant that he was on a short fuse. 'For heaven's sake!' he exploded. 'Why the iceberg look? Is it suddenly a crime to offer help? Do you realise how weird you are, Lauren Frazer?'

She was as tired as he was, and suddenly she too was spilling over with anger. 'And do you realise how obtuse you are? How many more times do I have to say that I want no patronage, no favours, no reason to be eternally damned grateful to anyone? I've had to be grateful all my life. It feels wonderful to be responsible for my own home, however poor. I can't think of anything I'd like less than to go back to owing it all to someone else again.'

He looked at her with displeasure. 'An attitude that seems to be unique to you. You certainly wouldn't be the first person to borrow from the business.'

'You make it sound so impersonal. . ."the business". But the business is *you* and I refuse to be indebted to you. To anyone—but particularly to you,'

He ran an angry hand through his hair, leaving it tousled.

'You make me sick. You could learn a lot from the kid whose tyre I changed earlier. She didn't go into a flat spin and send me on my way. She was actually normally, healthily grateful.'

'I'm aware of that. There are traces of her gratitude on your face,' Lauren said cuttingly. In the brightness of the kitchen she could see that the mark on his cheek was a smear of pink lipstick.

His hand went unerringly to the spot and rubbed the evidence away. A combination of anger and exhaustion made his face seem carved from granite, the flesh spare and taut over the bones of his skull. 'I bet you've never in your life felt enough warmth to want to fling your arms round someone and give them a kiss,' he said vehemently. 'And I'm damned sure no man has ever been encouraged to do the same to you.'

Lauren headed for the door. 'Speculate as much as you like. You're not going to pry into that aspect of my private life under the guise of making me a better functioning employee of Spencer Travis.'

At the door, as she stepped aside to let him out, he paused and looked her in the face. 'You could end up a sour old maid with little more than a cat to keep you company.'

'There are worse prospects—and plenty of teenage motorists.' Her eyes went deliberately to the side of his face that still had the faint pink mark on it.

His eyes blazed, but his voice was controlled as he said, 'Ever read Andrew Marvell? Watch out for "deserts of vast eternity". You seem a prime candidate for the worms that "shall try that long-preserved virginity".'

'I've lost track somewhere in the course of this conversation,' Lauren said scathingly. 'I thought we were talking about whether or not I wished to borrow money.'

She closed the door quickly and then had to sit down, appalled at the way the atmosphere had deteriorated. What on earth had got into the pair of them? They were both tired, admittedly, but how had it all got so out of hand? One minute he was offering her the working treat of a lifetime and she was accepting with joy. The next, they were hurling insults at each other in a way that she at least had never behaved before.

Now, she couldn't picture his face without that smear of pink lipstick on it. Was she crazy enough to be jealous? Jealous of some incompetent kid who

thought he was Sir Galahad and rewarded him accord-
ingly? It was nothing—a mere triviality. But a triviality
that he had seemed damned smug about.

Would they ever manage to face each other and
forget it? Put it all down to overwork and a general
feeling of being at the end of one's tether? It was to be
hoped so.

On Monday she went in to the office at seven-thirty
and personally saw to the duplicating of the material
she had typed up so that she could leave the copies on
Charles' desk and avoid seeing him. His secretary,
recovered and back at work, phoned to pass on his
thanks. He was obviously as little inclined towards a
personal encounter as Lauren was.

But when she arrived home that night her neighbour
brought round a huge and most beautiful pale peach
azalea, hand-delivered, gift-wrapped and ribbon-
bedecked, with a note attached in the bold black script
Lauren knew so well.

She could almost hear his voice as her eyes followed
the words. 'A million thanks for your help, without
which the weekend would have been indescribably
worse. Charles.'

Lauren placed the plant on her treasured mahogany
stand in the sitting-room which it had been so discern-
ingly bought to match and enhance, then she perched
on the sofa, hugging her knees, resting her chin on
them as she stared at the azalea.

Smoothly done, Charles Lennox, she thought. Now
I can thank you pleasantly for the plant when I next
see you, and neither of us need mention that awful
evening. Cleverly managed, as usual.

It was such a beautiful azalea. . . The unfortunate
side-effect was that she couldn't help thinking of its
donor every time her eyes fell on it. But that, no
doubt, would fade, as would the plant.

*   *   *

Paul's seat on the Caribbean flight next to Lauren's was still empty and take-off time was alarmingly close. When he hadn't turned up in the departure lounge, she had tried to phone his home or Charles' or the Banbury office, but had not got further than the computerised 'busy lines to London' announcement. Now she was feverishly imagining how on earth she would cope with the course single-handed in a way that would justify the expense of it, which, given the prestige location, was high. She was looking anxiously out of the window when he felt someone sit heavily in the seat next to hers.

'Thank heavens you made it! What happened?' She turned thankfully to see Charles, not Paul, looking at her, and felt as though she had been kicked in the stomach. 'What's going on?' she said, her voice changing.

Charles let his head sink back against the seat, long dark lashes shuttering those arresting green eyes.

'Paul's gone down with that damned flu bug. Phoned me in the small hours. I've had the devil's own job to get here and sort out the paperwork to take his place.'

The seatbelts warning came over the intercom. The engine noise rose to its peak roar. Lauren was silent.

The plane taxied the length of the runway and turned to gather speed.

'The last thing I want at this point,' Charles said, his voice discreetly low but not so low that she couldn't detect the iron note in it, 'is a prima-donna demonstration of how much you don't like the change in arrangements. This is the way it is, and you will cut the cold war immediately and put on the sort of face our clients are entitled to expect for their money. Is that understood?'

'I'm not thinking about you,' Lauren said between gritted teeth. 'I've never flown before. I'm *terrified*!'

He turned his head and saw her white face, the

prominent knuckles on her hands as she gripped the
arm-rests.

'That, at least, I can deal with,' he said. He gently
detached the nearest of her hands and folded it in his
own. 'Do you imagine that I would allow anything to
happen to a plane full of clients, myself, and you?' he
asked in a no-nonsense voice full of comforting if
unfounded self-assurance. 'This is the troublesome bit.
Another few minutes and it's magic. You'll see.'

The plane began to lift, and Lauren's fingers tightened convulsively on his as she clung to both voice and
hand while his thumb gently investigated the contours
of her wrist.

'I would have let you know what was going on,'
he said, determinedly talking her through the pressure
of take-off, 'but Paul was so feverish he couldn't
find your number. I'm rather worried about how he's
going to cope. I've left a note for the woman who
comes in to my place to go over and see what she can
do for him. He said he'd phone his doctor this
morning.'

Her need for an anchor to the world she was soaring
away from subsided. The soft, silken slide of his thumb
over her inner wrist was beginning to awake startling
awareness of an erotic zone she had no idea existed
before this moment. Dazed by it, she was reminded
that she was once again turning into the sort of clinging
vine she had no intention of being, and withdrew her
hand self-consciously.

'You must have had quite a night,' she managed to
say.

He glanced down at her. 'One that makes me think
Grenada owes me a good time. Better now?'

'Wary, but more or less back inside my head.'

'Good.' He gave her an extremely firm look. 'Now,
Lauren Frazer, I hope you're not going to turn into
the sort of idiot who refuses to enjoy this lovely island

we're going to just because the arrangements have changed?'

'I'm not quite such an idiot as that. I intend to enjoy every minute!' she said indignantly.

He gave a satisfied nod of approval. 'That's that settled, then. Now. . .if you feel up to it, let's go over the course details.'

'Ready when you are.' Work took over, but her wrist still tingled, sending a faint, delicious tremor up her arm.

The Tamarind was a small jewel of a hotel complex, taken over entirely by Charles and his party, and the first sight of it took Lauren's breath away.

Clustered round curving, dazzlingly white sands and poised on terraces up the lush, green, steeply sloping hillside were twenty or so individual cottages. In the centre of the bay was the Spanish-style main building where, under the glowing red tiles of the roof, the wide white arches of the reception area, ballroom, lounge and restaurant were open to glorious views over the sea. The rooms where the courses would be held were prudently sited at the rear, though still overlooking the potential distraction of grounds simply exploding with vivid, tropical flowers and studded with the jewel-like flash and hover of tiny humming-birds.

Lauren's cottage was one of three flanking a private swimming pool screened by the carnation-like blooms of oleanders and the vivid red petals of hibiscus. Charles was in the cottage facing Lauren's across the pool, the director of the firm in the cottage between them. That, she thought, seemed safe enough.

The cool air-conditioning was welcome after the hot afternoon sun. In her bedroom with its two antique four-poster beds Lauren stripped off the suit she had worn for the journey and padded through to the bathroom where she ran cool water into the sunken Italian mosaic bath and laughed delightedly as she experimented with the various jets. There was going to be so much to do this week. Not routine 'do-it-everywhere' holiday pursuits, but things that could only mean Grenada. There was to be a day cruise to the nearest of the Grenadines, the opportunity to swim in the crater of an extinct volcano, now a peaceful lake—even a chance to bathe in the pool at the foot of the island's most celebrated waterfall. . .though how on earth she would tear herself away from that glorious seashore in any spare time that there was, she couldn't imagine.

Refreshed, she put on a burnt-orange sarong dress which, in this setting, looked just right against the glossy darkness of her hair, with white flower cluster earrings and delicate strappy sandals to complete the picture. It was still three quarters of an hour to the time for the welcome dinner, and Charles had said there was no need to go over to the restaurant early. Framed in the window that overlooked the balcony, the sea beckoned. Lauren answered its call.

The water was clear and sparkling, simply dancing with sunshine. It was like looking down into a giant aquamarine gemstone. Lauren stood poised at the edge where white frills of waves murmured up to her feet, longing for tomorrow and her first chance to plunge in and feel the water's warm, silken caress.

'Are you going to jump in fully clad?' an amused voice asked, and Lauren turned to see Charles leaning against the soaring trunk of a palm tree to her right. Her heart did its usual forbidden flip at the sight of him, devastatingly handsome as always in his ivory jeans and olive silk shirt that echoed the colour of his eyes—eyes that were making no secret of the fact that they were taking in every detail of her own appearance and liking what they saw.

She forced down the ripple of gratification at his undisguised pleasure and attempted to speak normally. 'I'm tempted. I can't wait for the first swim tomorrow.'

'This place will do for the next few days, then?'

'Nowhere could be more lovely. You know the island well?'

'I've been coming here for years.'

'Lucky you!'

'By the end of the week you'll know it well too. I'll make sure of that.' Again the green eyes made a leisurely journey over her in a way that made her feel as though she was in the full heat of the sun again in spite of the blue shimmering haze of evening that was beginning to gather. 'You look delightful in that colour.' His voice was warm, dangerously husky.

Response stirred in her again, this time more strongly. She banished it. 'Bit of a gypsy look, really. But I'm still the same old traditional me in spite of the exotic trappings.'

'Is that a warning for me, or for yourself?' Was there the hint of threat in his smile?

She gave a little shrug. 'Just a statement of fact. Isn't it time we went over to join the others?'

'We'll see what a rum punch does for the gypsy. I warn you, there's enough kick and nutmeg in them to blow your hat off. Steady! You haven't had it yet!'

Turning unwarily, Lauren had almost tripped over a conch shell and was steadied by Charles' hand on her arm. He only held her briefly until she had regained her balance, but it was long enough for the soft flesh he had touched to throb with the illusion of burning under what she knew in her head had been the cool imprint of his fingers. Fire and ice, she thought incoherently. Both of them dangerous.

In the bar she watched him reflectively as he stood chatting to the barman while the rum punches were mixed. His tall figure was dynamic, even in casual clothes, his fascinating face relaxed. But could she relax? Could she be certain that he didn't have plans, other than the working ones she had already gone through with him, for this week? She could sense already that the island had a heady, exotic atmosphere—one that could lower barriers and weave dangerous magic. She must be on her guard.

Her eyes went to the bay, where a rose-red sky silhouetted the soaring elegance of the palms, while lights twinkled like jewels in the exotic vegetation. It was such a beautiful place. They were not alone. Surely nothing could happen here—unless she wanted it to. Enough of these eternal doubts and fears. How could she do other than enjoy herself in such a paradise?

Charles saw the smile playing round her lips. 'I always suspected that your face was made for smiling.' He handed Lauren her glass of punch and touched his own glass to it. 'To a happy week ahead.'

'This is what I have to be wary of?' she enquired as her eyes met his, and realised too late that her words could apply to the punch or to the week ahead.

Before he could answer, a bunch of their students came laughing in, in party mood and holiday clothes, and the evening took off.

At the end of the first lecture and training session she organised, and which Charles attended as she attended all his groups, he waited until all the students had filtered away in the direction of their cottages and walked back to their section of the grounds with Lauren.

'That was first-rate,' he told her. 'I was absolutely right to take you on board.'

Because the compliment pleased her, she brushed it aside.

'I hope I'm capable.' Her matter-of-factness cost her an effort. 'I would hate to let Paul down. I wonder how he is?'

'Recovering, I imagine.' It wasn't said in a tone of sympathy. He sounded impatient as he added, 'You know he's a confirmed bachelor?'

She looked at Charles in surprise. 'Is he? Well, that's his business, not mine.'

'It would be very much your business if you allowed your gratitude for the fact that he gave you a job to get out of hand.'

'What *do* you mean by that?' They had both stopped and were now facing each other.

'I mean that it's as well to spell things out. You're something of an novice when it comes to male-female relationships.'

Colour flooded her sun-kissed cheeks. 'Paul and I don't have a male-female relationship. He's my boss.'

'I thought you were only too aware that working together doesn't prevent relationships forming.'

'Oh, stop making something out of nothing,' she said crossly. 'And stop trespassing on what should be private territory. I'm mature enough to handle my own life.'

'You *look* mature enough.' He didn't touch her, but it was as though he did as his eyes travelled slowly from her glossy dark head down over the clinging white silk shirt and jade linen skirt to the coral-lacquered nails on her slim brown feet. 'My eyes do an excellent job of convincing me of the maturity of your outward appearance. But here——' now he did reach out and slowly run his fingers across her forehead— 'and here——' the lightest of lingering touches over her heart '—how mature are you in those areas, Lauren? You're not going to stop me calling a halt if I see you rushing like a lemming in the wrong direction. However, you assure me that that is not the case with Paul. End of subject for the time being. Coming for a swim before lunch?'

'I'm meeting someone in the bar,' she said, the fire of his touch burning her brow and her breast. She was longing for the sea, but not with him. Not after that.

She had promised to meet no one, but it didn't take long for the one person she had already picked out as potential trouble to latch on to her. He was the youngest of their client firm's salesmen, with all the go-getting woman-hunting attitude of the species, and it wasn't long before she realised that, far from being a safe harbour from the constant threat that Charles seemed to be, Darrell Jones was all set to shepherd her enthusiastically from frying-pan to fire.

Unable to avoid going in to lunch with him, Lauren managed to shake him off during the free afternoon hours. But the pursuit continued at the dancing that evening, and though she made attempts to get away from him, he doggedly shadowed her, catching her hand, slipping an arm round her waist, holding her far too close when the music changed to slow tempo. He ruined the gentle music of the steel band, and made the air heavy with the scent of spices seem cloying.

Charles knew what was going on, but she imagined he was not averse to see her in trouble of her own making and thought it would teach her a lesson. And she had, after all, told him that she didn't want his supervision.

In the end Lauren slipped prudently back to her cottage while Darrell was at the bar, congratulating herself on avoiding an even more disastrous ending to the evening.

She was dismayed when she came out of the bathroom in her thin cotton robe to see a dim figure coming up the steps of her private terrace, the moonlight glinting on the two glasses in his hands.

'Good idea to have a quiet last drink, no?' Darrell said thickly, putting the glasses down on the table.

'No, thanks. I'm tired. I'm going to bed,' she said firmly.

A lascivious grin spread across his face. 'I don't mind that as an alternative.' His hot hands pawed clumsily at her.

Lauren attempted to freeze him out, rigid and

unresponsive. 'Don't waste your time. Take your drinks and go back to the party.'

'Rather be here. C'mon! Just an itsy-bitsy kiss.' His moist lips made her flesh creep. 'Look at that moon. Lovers' moon!'

His intention was obvious as his breathing intensified and his hands stopped holding and began to explore.

They were alone here—and in any case, the possibility of bringing anyone else in on such a scene was unbearable. Lauren forgot about freezing and began to fight his clumsy drunken passion like a wildcat, but it only served to excite him more.

Suddenly a voice spoke out of the darkness, cutting into the sordid scene with calm, crisp authority. Charles' voice.

'I think you got it slightly wrong, Darrell. Let's be sensible and leave the lady in peace, shall we? She's tired.'

'Only a bit of fun,' the erstwhile assailant mumbled, transformed by discovery and the impact of Charles' huge, sober presence into a harmless kid who had drunk rather too much.

'Of course. Better if the fun's mutual, though. These yours?' Charles scooped up the two glasses and turned Darrell adroitly towards the steps. 'Come on, then. I'll walk back with you and let you into a little secret. Mind the step. We don't want you getting hurt, do we?'

He had not looked directly at Lauren, who felt totally humiliated but incredibly thankful for once that he had stuck his aristocratic nose into her unfortunate business on this occasion. She was shaking, and when they had disappeared she helped herself to a brandy, which she hated, to stiffen up her dissolving backbone.

There were footsteps in a few minutes, and Charles' voice calling out softly, 'Only me. Are you all right?'

'Getting better by the minute,' Lauren said, her pale face not backing up the words. 'Where is he?'

'Being safely tucked up for the night by his friends.' He sat in the white cane chair near the door, apart from her, not threatening by coming close, and she was grateful for his intuitive thoughtfulness. 'You don't have to worry. He won't be back.'

Lauren's teeth chattered against the rim of her glass. 'Sorry. Would you like a drink?' she asked.

'No, thanks. As soon as I'm sure you're not going to slide out of that chair in a faint, I'll be off. I imagine you've had enough of male company for today.'

'Enough of his,' she said with distate.

'It doesn't really pay to get too friendly with clients. They tend to think the money they pay covers a multitude of things.'

She shuddered, but managed a rueful smile. 'Lesson learned. How did you get rid of him so easily?'

'I have the size to make him think twice about turning nasty—unlike you. And once I got him away from you, I made sure he won't come sniffing round again by telling him that though we don't make it obvious when we are carrying out work schedules, you and I are rather more than working colleagues, and while one lapse from grace can be forgiven, I would take a dim view of any repetition.'

Lauren stared at him, speechless.

He grinned. 'It will work, believe me. And it's the lesser of two evils as far as you're concerned. Better safe in my company than sorry in the company of over-sexed young animals like Jones. In any case, I can't spend all my time wondering who's going to be chasing you home and up to no good once the sun goes down.' He stood up. 'You look rather more as though you'll live. Get to bed.'

She rose bemusedly, instinctively tightening the sash of her cotton robe. 'Well, thank you for tonight's rescue—I think.'

His shadowy green eyes slowly scanned her face.

'You're a silly, misguided girl, you know.' He smiled. 'Goodnight, Lauren.'

'Goodnight.' She locked the door after him, and leaned against it, thinking how exactly right his behaviour had been, and how very nice he seemed. . . sometimes. But there was more than one girl around who would claim otherwise. And she had had a father—though those were hardly appropriate words to describe the purely biological relationship—whose behaviour underlined the fact that it was fundamental attitude, not surface charm, that counted.

All the same, because she knew the togetherness was contrived for a purpose, Lauren relaxed into the safety of Charles' company. Relationships flared and waned among the students and several pretty island girls appeared regularly in the evenings for the dancing. Lauren watched with interest, glad to be safely detached from it all.

There were two free days at the end of the week's course, and when Charles suggested taking her over to the Grenadines in a boat he intended hiring, she felt sufficiently sure of him to agree. It was a once-in-a-lifetime opportunity, she told herself. She would be a fool to miss out on it.

Then, on the last communal night, everything was ruined.

Charles walked her back to her cottage in the early hours towards the end of the last-night party. It was the most luminous of nights, and the end of an out-of-this-world week added piquancy. She looked up at him, his profile in dramatic silhouette against the huge moon, and a painful ache of dissatisfaction filled her. The night and the place were perfect, but they demanded more than this somehow unconcluded ending of the evening. All the ingredients were there: moonlight and beauty, scents and distant, soft sounds of music and laughter, a man and a woman. . . But

the wrong man and woman. Two people incapable of
adding the final touch of perfection to the night. Two
people who were killing its beauty with a matter-of-
fact run-down of instructions for the following day,
none of which she found she could remember, while
inside her was this yearning for an indefinable something more, something that she knew perfectly well
was out of reach.

It was as though he read something of what she was
feeling in her eyes as they stopped below the terrace
of her bungalow. She saw the flash of awareness in his,
felt an almost tangible heightening of the tension she
had been aware of as they walked back. Her heart felt
as if it were swelling in her breast, pressing on her
lungs and constricting her breathing, blocking her
throat.

'What are we doing?' he asked softly, his hands
reaching out towards her. She wanted him as she had
never wanted any man. She was within a hair's breadth
of giving in to the turmoil of feeling inside her.

Fear exploded in her, saving her.

'Talking too much,' she said, then turned and ran
like the wind up the steps into her cottage.

Leaning against the door, weak with the danger she
had only just managed to escape from, she knew he
was standing there at the foot of the steps, motionless.
After what seemed like an eternity, footsteps marked
his departure, and she drew in a shuddering breath
and made herself begin packing, though she felt
drained of the necessary energy.

It was when she automatically went on to check
tickets and passport that Lauren realised she had
forgotten to pick up her bag when she left the ballroom. It seemed like the last straw, but there was
nothing for it but to set off back through the moonlit
grounds.

She had not gone far when she heard male voices
talking on a path that crossed the one on which she

was walking. One was Charles, she realised with a stab of fear. The other Darrell Jones, who had spent most of the evening in fierce rivalry with a colleague for the company of a young Caribbean girl. She couldn't bear the thought of confronting Charles again, and slipped into the shadows to wait until they had crossed the intersection and moved out of her path.

'Lauren's called it a day, then?' That was Darrell's voice.

'She has. We have an early start tomorrow.' Charles sounded matter-of-fact, normal. Had she dreamed what happened?

There was a little pause, then Darrell spoke again.

'Our little strategy seemed to work, didn't it? You're a devious bastard, Lennox!'

Charles laughed. 'I learned early in my career that it's often surprisingly easy to get your own way by roundabout means.'

'Especially with women?'

'I didn't say that specifically.'

'No, but you've fiendishly well demonstrated it— with a little expert help from me, I might add!'

'I'll wait until the holiday's well and truly over before congratulating myself.' More male laughter. The voices became an indistinct murmur and the footsteps faded away.

Lauren, pressed against the rough bark of a palm tree, was devastated by what she had heard. Over and over the words she went, but each time they added up to the same humiliating meaning. 'Our little strategy,' Darrell had said. And Charles had laughed in that satisfied, knowing way. It could only mean that the pair of them had cooked up the mock attack and rescue situation earlier in the week, simply so that Charles, the 'devious bastard', could spend as much time as he wanted with her. And he was counting on the rest of the time before the return flight to get to the point where congratulations were in order.

Anger rose, bubbling up inside her, anger against herself as much as against him. She had fallen for it hook, line and sinker. And with interest—because she had been lulled into feeling so safe with him that she had agreed to go off alone with him tomorrow. She had even—and this was the most humiliating admission of all—she had even ached with longing to be in his arms less than an hour ago.

White-faced, she collected her bag and back in her room spent a grimly determined few minutes on the phone to the airport. It would cost her a travel supplement, but she got a flight transfer. Charles Lennox would learn that she might be gullible, but she was not a complete fool. Instead of being taken off for whatever island liaison he had in mind, she would be on her way home tomorrow, and he could go whistle for his holiday entertainment.

But what hurt like hell was the exact nature of that unbearable yearning outside her cottage in the spice-scented moonlight. She had not been wishing that he was someone different, or that she was a girl with a different past. She, with full knowledge of her origins, had wanted Charles—the man he was—to make love to her. It was as humiliating as that. And now she had to swallow the bitter fact that she had been brought to that point of desire by nothing more romantic than a cold-blooded plan cooked up by a couple of randy men.

Hot tears of frustration punctuated what was left of the night before her taxi collected her for the airport.

She left no message. Charles could explain her absence from the general departure tomorrow in any way he chose. Heaven knew he was capable of the necessary invention, she thought painfully.

CHAPTER SEVEN

LAUREN had expected a moment of reckoning and was not surprised when Charles appeared like an avenging angel on her doorstep in Cherwell Terrace, the dank November river mist swirling around him. But she had a sinking, despairing feeling when she discovered that the dark, beautiful planes of his face still had the power to twist and speed her heart in spite of what she knew.

'You owe me an explanation.'

'I owe you nothing.' She began to close the door and his arm reached out and stopped it effortlessly.

'Unless you want the whole terrace to hear, you had better ask me in.'

Lauren stood back silently and he strode past her into the warmth of the sitting-room, taking up a challenging stance in front of the fire, arms folded, chin jutting aggressively. His eyes narrowed and reflecting his mood, were a darkly threatening olive.

She was desparate to get him out of her territory. He seemed to fill the room, charging the atmosphere of it with the anger that she could feel coming towards her.

'I presume your hasty departure from Grenada was deliberately calculated to make me look an idiot?' he erupted. 'I can think of no other reason for the total lack of communication.'

'*I* was the idiot—in your estimation,' she told him coldly from the doorway, reluctant to leave the advantage of the deep step down into the sitting-room. 'I heard your conversation in the grounds of the Tamarind with Darrell Jones on the night I left.'

'What the hell has Darrell Jones got to do with

anything? And how could any conversation I had with him be relevant to your bolting for home without the courtesy of a single word?'

His acting was admirable, she had to give him that. It would be easy to think that he was as puzzled as he was pretending to be. But she had had first-hand experience of his acting on Grenada, hadn't she? It was less effective second time around.

She looked stonily at him. 'Think back to the last-night party, after you'd walked me back to the cottage. You met Darrell then and had the conversation that surely explains everything now you know I overheard it.'

His brow furrowed. 'I met Darrell, yes. I spoke to him for a few minutes.' He appeared to be racking his memory. 'I can recall the conversation—it wasn't long. But I'm damned if I can think why it had such a dramatic effect on you.'

Lauren's colour rose. 'Then let me spell it out. You both referred to me by name, and to the strategy—the "effective little strategy" you'd cooked up—which seemed to cause a certain amusement. It wasn't hard to realise which little strategy that was. Darrell the drunken molesting villain, you the knight in shining armour—and myself the sucker who fell victim to both? Darrell called you a devious bastard. For once I couldn't agree with him more—but I'd apply the description to the pair of you. A tawdry trick, Charles. Even knowing your reputation, I'd have thought you above it.'

He was looking at her in complete astonishment now.

'Just a minute! If you imagine we were talking about a strategy concerning you, you couldn't be more wrong.'

'You fooled me once. You'll not do it again,' she said curtly.

'Listen, can't you?' he thundered. 'Stop putting

yourself in the centre of the picture. Think back. Don't you remember the three-cornered struggle between Darrell, one of the other men, and a young native girl whose mother should never have allowed her out?'

'What has that to do with anything?' Lauren said impatiently.

'It's extremely relevant. I saw that things were getting rather too hot for the age of the girl, and I suggested to Darrell—who thought he had good reason to be grateful for not getting into more serious bad books with me, if you remember——' here he directed a furious glare at Lauren '—that a bit of competition for Latisha's attention was called for. Trouble-shooting dangerous relationships isn't written into the contract, but it features on my private agenda, as you should know.' Slowly, menacingly he came towards her, each sentence punctuated by a step narrowing the gap between them. 'That was the little strategy referred to. Nothing to do with you—apart from a cursory enquiry as to your whereabouts at the start of the conversation. Absolutely damn-all to do with this precious virtue of yours. You twisted our words to fit the contorted corridors of your suspicious little mind. Why don't you stop imagining that every decent man in creation is out to deflower you and concentrate on sussing out the real villains?'

'Full marks for your power of invention!' she blustered, unwilling to give in to the conviction that he was speaking the truth.

'I don't have any inventing to do,' he amended curtly. 'That's your sphere. You deprived yourself of two enjoyable days in the Caribbean because you've got an over-fertile imagination and a huge chip on your shoulder.' His eyes flashed, a fiery emerald now. 'But there's a third reason for your reacting so strongly to what you thought you heard, isn't there?'

'If there is, I expect you'll tell me,' she said defiantly.

'Yes, I'll tell you.' A nerve leapt in his cheek. 'What

really bugged you was the fact that only a few minutes before you read so much into an innocent conversation, you'd actually been desperate for me to kiss you, hadn't you?' he said. 'You'd been trembling on the verge of coming alive for a fragile moment, but living doesn't enter into Lauren Frazer's scheme of things, does it?'

'Stop it!' she interjected harshly. 'You're wrong!'

He seized her shoulders and thrust his face within inches of hers, his breath hot on her. 'Admit it!'

'No! There's nothing to admit!' She was struggling, squirming, kicking, but he only held her more tightly.

'There is—and you will. But it doesn't have to be in words.'

Then he was kissing her, and in the seconds it took for the harsh attack of his lips to soften into infinitely more dangerous gentleness, she was lost. Anger, hurt pride, fear, all drained away. How can he do this to me? she thought desperately for the split-second before a slow, deep shudder went rippling through her, leaving in its wake a quivering ache that only Charles could heal. Her arms had somehow found their way round him and her fingers were cradling the nape of his neck. She was lost in the feel and the taste and the familiar clean, male scent of him. The build-up to the kiss, the original reason for it, her resistance, all were forgotten, blown away as though they had never been. Her blood was racing, her heart thundering, her flesh melting against him.

When his mouth at last released hers, her choked, murmuring cry of protest came from the sheer pain of deprivation. They stared feverishly into each other's eyes.

'Now argue that away,' he said passionately.

Lauren drew in a ragged breath, closing her eyes against the knowledge in his.

'Please go,' she said faintly.

'Feeling threatened again?' he hurled at her. Then,

roughly, 'Think about it, Lauren. That kiss. Decide what you're going to do about it. Delude yourself if you can that it meant nothing.'

The door closed softly behind him. Lauren sank into the nearest chair. She had never felt like that in her life. The terrifying power generated by his kiss had seemed to split every atom of her being, unleashing an equally dangerous force in herself. He could have kissed her into doing anything.

Was it in the blood? Had her mother felt like that? She shivered. She hadn't known. . .hadn't dreamed how powerful emotion could be. It was mind-blowing, will-shattering, resolution-blasting. She wanted her head to rule her life, but how was that possible when flesh and blood could be such tyrants?

If he had insisted on staying—would she, could she have prevented the happening of something that seemed such an inevitable consequence during those wild, incandescent seconds with every part of her greedily crying out for more?

To stay on in his employment would indicate her tacit acceptance of the feelings he knew he had aroused in her. . .even her willingness to risk things going further. And if she didn't delude herself about her own feelings, neither could she fool herself about his. He was a man renowned for staying the course as far as the point of satisfaction, but not as far as the point of commitment.

She would not run the risk of following her mother's pattern. She would not.

If only she could turn the clock back. Before she became involved with Charles Lennox, the answer to this kind of situation had seemed simple. You walked away from it. Now there was something inside her that made that simple solution sheer torture to implement. But there was no other way. Somehow, between now and tomorrow, she had to summon up the will to cut herself free from a job she loved, and a man who, in spite of all she knew about him, could still create this havoc in her.

Next day, she found that she had five days in which to think more calmly about an alternative future for herself. Charles was in London until the following Monday.

Paul was back, and fit. Life for everyone in the office apart from herself seemed normal.

'You don't look as though your time in the Caribbean did you much good,' Paul said frankly. 'Not going down with flu, are you?'

'Just paying for being away. There's masses to catch up on,' she told him, knowing that it was the decision hanging over her, not work, that was responsible for the pallor beneath her tan.

A phone call from Marian, her counterpart in the London office, underlined that Lauren was right to leave. Business out of the way, Marian's voice lowered. 'Bit of scandal for you. I'm not giving any secrets away. I got it from a tabloid someone brought into the office, so it's public knowledge. Did you know that Charles backed out of marriage with a girl called Imogen Carpenter?'

'That's old news. I heard it before I joined Spencer Travis.' Lauren was uncomfortable with Marian's gossipy tone.

'Well—she's pregnant—dating from the appropriate time by the looks of it. He's made the gossip column again, and had a face like a thundercloud ever since the paper came out yesterday. Apparently some photographer happened to be around when they met up while he's been in London this last day or two, and there they are in the paper, one obviously pregnant woman, and one worried man. The caption was, "City tycoon Charles Lennox at lunch with his recently jilted fiancée, Imogen Carpenter". All they need to say, really. It's a very clear picture. The conclusions to draw are obvious.'

'And the whole world's ready to draw them,' Lauren said with difficulty, sickened by this further evidence of what kind of man she had managed to fall in love with.

'Yes! Rotten lot, aren't we?' Marian said, unabashed. 'Anyway, I thought you should know, if no one's passed it round the Banbury office. Watch out for his lordship's temper. Judging by the cyclone that went through this place today, he's going to need careful handling.'

Lauren went to the agency in her lunch-hour. She took the only interview on offer, for a temporary job nowhere near good enough, determined to take it if given the chance. Desperate times, desperate measures. And no times could be more desperate than hers.

The summons to the managing director's office came just after nine on the morning of Charles' return. Lauren, tense and pale-faced with the knowledge that her letter of resignation, put on Charles' desk first thing that morning, had presumably been read, walked up to the top floor.

'Care to give me another overdue explanation?' Charles said, brandishing her letter crisply at her as soon as she appeared in the doorway. The words were casual. His eyes were anything but. 'Come in and close the door,' he added impatiently.

Lauren did just that, remaining with her back against the polished wood.

'That as far as you dare come?'

'I don't anticipate a long stay,' she told him quietly.

His eyes were cold as green ice. 'For the moment you are in my employment. Come and sit down.'

'It won't make an atom of difference,' Lauren said, but as he made a move to rise she hurriedly complied.

He stared across the desk at her. He looked tired

and strained as well as angry. The days in London had
taken their toll, but no doubt Imogen Carpenter was
feeling equally despairing. 'I take it that our last
meeting was too much for your sensibilities,' he said
harshly. 'I can think of no other reason for this
nonsense.'

Lauren flushed. 'There's no point in talking about
it. It happened—and I've reacted. End of story.'

'Reacted stupidly.'

'In the way that seemed most appropriate to me.
That's my right.' Her eyes blazed at him. 'The decent
thing would have been to leave it at telling me what a
wrong conclusion I'd jumped to. But you weren't
satisfied with that. You had to go further.'

His eyes narrowed. 'You didn't give me the
impression of being averse to the experience at the
time.'

'You proved that I make mistakes. I made another,'
she said bitterly.

'And now you're about to compound it.' He was
sliding his fingers down the length of the pen, inverting
it, repeating the whole process time after time. The
tap-tap-tap of it on the desk pounded on her nerves. 'I
was angry,' he said explosively. 'Who wouldn't be, to
have someone run out on them like that?'

'Perhaps it won't hurt you to discover what it's like
to be walked out on. You've done it often enough.'

A blaze of fury flared across his face. 'Let's leave
your idea of my past out of it, shall we? Your own
present is quite enough to be going on with.' He got
up and walked the length of the office and back again
to stand over her. 'What you are doing is insane.'

'You're wasting your time, Charles. I'm leaving.'

He strode round his chair and flung himself into it.

'You're forgetting one important factor. Your
contract.'

'I haven't forgotten. It falls due for renewal at the

end of the period of notice I've given. I don't wish to renew it.'

'Then have you forgotten that you may not find it easy to get another job?'

'I don't have to worry about that. I've already got one.'

He went very still. 'May I ask what it is?' he asked dangerously quietly.

'I'm replacing someone who is going on maternity leave.'

'A temporary post? I can't believe this!'

'Yes. But I know my worth. A temporary post may lead to something more permanent once I'm through the door,' she told him.

'And are you replacing someone in a managerial position comparable to the one you have held here?'

She swallowed. 'I didn't expect a managerial position.'

'Then what type of job have you exchanged your present responsible one for, may I ask?'

'Secretarial,' she said abruptly.

His chair scraped angrily back. 'Hell's bells, Lauren! Do you mean to tell me that after all you have done here, you're content to revert to the position of office dogsbody?'

'I'm happy to take this job.'

'Congratulations!' he said with bitter scorn. 'How to get from the top of the hill to the bottom in one easy move. You're a fool!'

'So you keep telling me. But not a big enough one to stay on here. Will that be all?' she asked, getting to her feet, the colour flaming in her cheeks now.

'One more thing. May I ask the name of the company for which you will be acting as secretary?'

'Univeral Management Services in Oxford. Fault that!'

She was sure he couldn't, and yet his face froze.

'Then I congratulate you. All becomes clear. I don't

doubt that you will have every chance to secure advancement for yourself.'

It was obvious that this was not an idle remark. 'Am I expected to understand what you mean by that?' Lauren asked.

His face seemed sculpted in steel. 'One of my rivals in the training field will be only too glad to tap the mind of someone who has inside knowledge of Spencer Travis' methods and clients.'

Lauren looked at him aghast. 'What do you think I am? That's a despicable implication.'

'How the hell do I know what you are?' he said icily. 'So far it's been one continuous, pitfall-bedevilled process of finding out, and right now I don't at all care for what I'm discovering.' His chair scraped back angrily as he rose. 'Don't bother to work your three months out. I prefer you to clear your desk today.'

There was a stunned silence. At last Lauren found her voice. 'Very well, if that's what you want.' Hurt swelled in her throat. 'But you're wrong. I couldn't possibly behave as you suggest.'

'Time will establish that, one way or another.' When she still hesitated, looking helplessly at him, horrified at such an ending, he looked coldly at her. 'That's all. More than enough. Please go.'

The memory of his tone and the look on his face stayed with her like the touch of winter as she went numbly downstairs.

Everyone was out of the office at Paul's weekly briefing in an adjoining room. Barely managing to control her feelings, Lauren was thankful to have the place to herself. She wrote Paul an indadequate note of apology for her abrupt departure, entirely defeated by the attempt to explain, then picked up her few personal effects and went downstairs, where the glass doors of Spencer Travis swung to behind her for the last time, even the girl on Reception unaware that she was not merely slipping out on business.

Leaving was what she wanted to do, she repeatedly told herself. It was the wise thing, the sensible thing, the only thing. But it didn't feel like it. It felt hollow and wretched and—thanks to Charles' quite wrong assumption about her—steeped in shame.

Wasn't there enough pain in the situation, she asked passionately, raging against the fate that had added this hurt to the rest. It was no use telling herself that it didn't matter what Charles thought of her. The plain truth was that it did. She knew what kind of man he was, what kind of life he had led, and yet she still cared what he thought of her. Could anything be more irrational?

He had called her a fool. He was right about that, at least.

She threw herself into a frenzy of painting and hanging wallpaper, desperate for time to pass until it was time to take up her new job.

Fate hadn't yet finished with her. Three days after she had left Spencer Travis, she received an apologetic call from the personnel officer at Universal Management Services. The girl Lauren was to replace had had a miscarriage. Her job would therefore not be available. The company was extremely sorry. They regretted that there were no other vacancies with them at the moment, though they would of course keep Lauren's details and be in touch if any opening occurred. They would be forwarding a month's salary as a token of their regret.

Lauren expressed dazed understanding of the circumstances, and put down the phone. So much for Charles' idea that Universal Management Services were eager to pick her brains. If that had been the case they would have found her some kind of place on the staff.

Strangely, she found that once the initial shock had worn off, she felt almost relieved. News got around, and though she wouldn't have dreamed of getting in touch with Charles to tell him how wrong he had been, that didn't mean that he wouldn't find out through mutual acquaintances. Her eyes fired at the prospect of his being made to feel like the heel he was.

Idiot! she berated herself immediately afterwards. You're one of the vast army of the unemployed, so what have you got to feel triumphant about? You've no reference from Spencer Travis, and no intention of crawling around begging for one, even if there was the remotest chance of one being given. Hardly best equipped to start on the agency trail again, are you?

But that was what she must do—and quickly.

The job front was bleak. Every agency had the same message. Just before Christmas was not the time to expect vacancies to occur.

'It takes almost to the end of January for people to get over the party season and summon up the energy to start moving again. It happens every year. But you can keep trying,' Lauren was told so many times that she had to believe it. She registered with all of them, then went into one of the town centre hotels to order coffee and a sandwich and have a good think. A series of depressing sums on the back of her cheque-book convinced her that things were going to be very tight indeed by the end of January, and that it would be rather better if Christmas didn't take place this year.

'Sorry you've had to wait so long,' the flushed-looking bar girl said, bringing her order. 'This place is bedlam—and it's going to get worse tonight. The manager's scarpered—with the evening bar girl, if you please! His wife doesn't know whether to hold the fort, pull the beers or have a nervous breakdown. You don't know anyone who might want to work in a madhouse, do you?'

It was meant as a joke, but to Lauren it seemed like the intervention of a more benign fate. Evenings earning at least *something* in the bar, with the rest of the day free to carry on job-hunting? It was too good an opportunity to miss after her painful accounting session, and she had done weekend bar work while she was at college, so the prospect didn't hold anything alarming.

'Do you know, I think I just might,' she told the waitress, and found out where she was likely to find the distraught manager's wife. By the time she left the hotel, she had got herself a temporary job, starting that same night.

It was inevitable that people she knew from Spencer Travis would come into the bar at some point. They were surprised to see her, of course, but seemed to accept that she was merely filling time until her new job started 'after Christmas', a loose statement which she hoped with all her heart would turn out to be true. Lauren was thankful she was too busy for long conversations. She had no idea what explanation of her abrupt departure had been circulated, and saw no point in trying to find out. The whole affair was unpleasant and embarrassing.

Late on Friday night, one of the busiest nights of her first week, Lauren cast an assessing glance over the crowds in the bar, and felt as though a thunderbolt had hit her when she found herself staring into the eyes of Charles Lennox. He had just come through the doors, and he looked as though the sight of her was as much a shock to him as his appearance was to her.

'See that man over by the entrance?' she said hurriedly to Beverley, the other girl on duty.

'The one just coming towards us? With the eyes?' Beverley said with graphic economy.

'That one. I don't want to serve him.'

'Strange girl! Your loss is my gain!'

'I mean it!' Lauren said urgently.

A bit of nifty footwork ensured that Beverley took

Charles' order while Lauren became studiously busy at the opposite end of the bar, but when he had picked up his drink he walked along and slipped into an empty space where Lauren, giving change to the customer next to whom Charles was now looming, couldn't avoid meeting his glacial green eyes.

'I want to speak to you,' he said baldly.

'I'm afraid I can't stop. People are waiting to be served,' Lauren told him, heart beating like fury, poised to move away.

'I can wait,' he told her ominously, and proceeded to do just that, a dark, threatening presence, his eyes on her, making her unnaturally clumsy and increasingly angry.

Customers thinned out, and the last drinks were served, the last glasses collected and washed. The moment could be put off no longer. Lauren buttoned on her red coat as though it were a suit of armour, and, looking straight ahead, made for the door, wishing desperately that she could bolt for the safety of her car in the car park. But her car was at home, having refused to start that evening, and she had the prospect of a walk to the bus stop and a wait of only minutes— but minutes that would seem like hours under the circumstances—for the late-night bus.

Charles was at her side before she reached the door, holding it open for her, looking like a gaoler escorting a prisoner back to the condemned cell.

'Where's your car?' he asked grimly.

'I haven't got it tonight.'

'How very fortunate. We can have a private talk while I drive you home.'

'I have no intention of being driven home,' she said curtly.

His hand gripped her elbow, steering her unflinchingly towards the Lotus. 'You are not being offered the choice.' He held the door open. 'Get in.'

Lauren considered and rejected the idea of an

undignified struggle. The door was closed on her sharply. Charles walked round and took his own seat. 'Now,' he said, 'perhaps you'll tell me what the hell you're up to, parading yourself as a barmaid.'

'May I rephrase that?' she retorted briskly. 'I'm earning myself a crust until it's time to start my new job.' The windscreen was frosted over, but she stared determinedly into its opaqueness.

'What new job?' The question was fired at her with the speed of a bullet, scepticism in each word.

'The job I shall be beginning after Christmas,' she hedged.

'Not at Universal Management, if my information is correct.'

She was jolted into looking at him, and immediately shocked by the fiery green eyes into looking away again. 'What do you mean?'

'Cut the pretence. You're not on their books. I checked.'

'What business is it of yours?' she said furiously. 'I ceased to be any concern of yours the moment I left Spencer Travis.'

'Then why have you taken a menial little job right where anyone from Spencer Travis can fall over you? Are you out to curry sympathy? Is the aim to make it as public as possible that I've more or less forced you to give up a job with a rival company and reduced you to pulling pints for a living?'

'How egotistic can you get!' Lauren blazed. 'No idiotic, false accusation of yours would make me give up anything. I'd be working at Universal Management right now if the girl I was scheduled to replace hadn't had a miscarriage and decided to go on working.'

'Then you didn't turn the job down because of what I said?'

'I did not! There wasn't a shred of truth in your offensive suggestion. Your rivals have obviously got higher standards than yourself. If they'd wanted to get information out of me, they'd have fitted me into the company somehow. But they didn't. They apologised and left it at that.'

'You mean they dropped you without any compensation?'

'I was compensated. They're not the kind of people to hire and fire indiscriminately. They wouldn't send someone packing in five minutes flat for perfectly spurious reasons,' she said accusingly.

'You made me angry. You have a greater talent for making me angry than anyone I know. Of course I realised that I had acted too precipitately, once I'd had the chance to cool down. And may I remind you that you resigned—I didn't fire you.'

'You didn't exactly fall over yourself to eat your words once you decided you'd "acted too precipitately".'

'I've been out of the country. I intended getting in touch. You aren't the only item on my agenda, you know.' There was a brief, sizzling silence. 'I do, of course, accept that while you may be foolish, you are not really the type to have criminal tendencies.'

'Big of you!' Lauren exploded. 'Nor am I the type to curry sympathy. I'm working at the Hamilton because that happens to be where the job is. Now that you know I'm there, perhaps you'll do me the favour of taking your custom elsewhere.'

'How long is that particular farce going to go on?'

'Until I find permanent work, obviously.'

'You're trying?'

'Of course I'm trying. That was the whole point of taking evening work.'

He breathed heavily for a moment, staring ahead as she was. 'I haven't replaced you—yet. In view of the mess you seem to have got yourself in, I feel duty bound to offer you your old job back.'

The offer was made as grudgingly as it was unwelcome. 'Don't give duty a second thought. There'd be snow in hell before I'd work at Spencer Travis again,' Lauren said decisively.

'Still as bent on self-destruction as ever, I see,' he said furiously. 'Stick at your pint-pulling, then. Who knows, you may rise to the dizzy heights of running your own pub one day.'

'That prospect is distinctly more pleasant than the thought of making the same mistake twice over. Perhaps you will now get on with the job of driving me home. I think we've covered all the points it's necessary to deal with,' Lauren said icily.

He started up the engine so fiercely that it was a miracle the key didn't snap in two in the lock, and drove out of the car park in fulminating silence, not speaking again until he drew up in Cherwell Terrace, where he opened the door for her to get out of his car and suddenly hurled at her, '*Why* are you so incapable of seeing sense?'

'Because I won't dance to your tune? I call that seeing very clearly indeed.'

'And I call it mulish short-sightedness.'

'Thank you for the lift,' she said politely. 'As for your opinion, I'd be rather more concerned if you thought well of me.'

He made an explosive comment which it was probably as well she couldn't quite hear, and slammed back into the car, the scream of the engine as he roared off down the road no doubt waking up half the neighbourhood.

Lauren let herself limply into her little house and went straight up to bed, too exhausted both physically and mentally to do anything else. She lay awake staring into the darkness for a long time, devastated by yet another fraught meeting with Charles Lennox. Then she tossed and turned fitfully, not sleeping really deeply until the early hours, when she sank into such deep slumber that, instead of waking at seven as she usually did, she was roused by the clatter of the letterbox an hour later.

It wasn't the postman, she found when she ran down the stairs, hoping as always that there might be good news in the post. A long white envelope had been delivered by hand.

She tore it open and two papers fell out, one typewritten, one handwritten. Charles' writing. She read the handwritten note first.

'I know what you said,' the forceful, sloping Italian script informed her, 'but you may find the enclosed useful. For God's sake don't be so ridiculous as to refuse to use it. You earned it, and I mean it. Charles.'

The other paper, closely typed at much greater length, was a testimonial to her brief time at Spencer Travis, written in such warm, glowing terms that when she had read it she sat down at the table, buried her head in her arms and burst into tears. She had wanted him to think well of her and, now that he had shown that he did, it gave her the most unbearable pain in her heart.

What a mixed-up creature she was, she thought at last, drained by her emotion. She couldn't bear the thought of being with him, and yet she felt only half a person away from him. She disapproved of him, and yet longed for his approval. She could cope with insults, but praise reduced her to this wailing wreck. She wanted her connection with him to be over, and yet now that he was underlining its conclusion by helping her to get another job, she felt as though she was drowning and he had thrown her a lifebelt only to cut the rope that would allow him to haul her back to him.

You've got to pull yourself together, she told herself harshly. The phone rang, and hope flared ridiculously in her again. Was it Charles? She flew across the room to answer it.

'Lauren? I think it's time we got together again, don't you?' Donna said, having, it seemed, decided to return Lauren's call at last.

CHAPTER EIGHT

SIMONETTO'S where Lauren and her cousin had arranged to meet for Saturday lunch, was a highly fashionable place.

'But it's a special occasion, after all. And this is my treat, I insist,' Donna had said surprisingly.

She was already there when Lauren arrived, and rose to give her an effusive hug. Hostilities were obviously over. Lauren, though as always slightly wary of her cousin, was glad of it. After all the years of family closeness, she had felt sad about the break in relations in spite of events that had caused it.

'Lovely to see you again!' Donna said now. 'I can't believe how many weeks have gone by. We should never have let time pass for so long without meeting. How've you been?'

'I'm well. How about you?' Lauren enquired.

'Busy. I can't tell you how rushed off my feet I am! But I mustn't grumble about that these days, must I? What about you? How's the job?'

Lauren didn't want to embark on the sorry story of her present circumstances. In spite of having her glowing reference, she had still not found work. In fact, she had not even managed to get an interview for the one vacancy that had come up in Oxford, and it was getting more and more worrying. The manager's wife at the Hamilton was showing every sign of bouncing back, too, and was interviewing next week for a permanent bar girl, so even the bar job wasn't going to last much longer.

'Fine!' she said brightly, and switched the conversation to Maggie and the Allardyce House staff.

They ordered, and while they waited for the food to

be brought, Donna said with sudden interest, 'Look who's over there, at the table by the window!'

Lauren gave a discreet glance, and was glad she was sitting down, otherwise the unexpected shock of seeing Charles felt as though it would have been strong enough to make her collapse. As it was, the kind of circulation-stopping sensation that looking down from great heights gave her ran through her. He was deep in conversation with his table companion, whom Lauren recognised as one of Spencer Travis' clients, a certain Roberta Dale. A client who didn't seem to be behaving in a particularly business-like manner at the moment. She was laughing into Charles' face with what appeared to be blatant seduction, and her hand was reaching across the table to touch his. A fierce wave of jealousy ran through Lauren. Why can't it be over for me? she asked herself fiercely.

'Who's he with, I wonder?' Donna speculated. 'Girl-friend? Must be. She can't keep her hands off him. Well, now we know he prefers blondes!'

'This week, at least!' Lauren said tersely. Before she left Spencer Travis, discussions had been taking place between Charles and Roberta Dale about an important training contract with the Dale family firm. It looked as though he was getting the business, she thought viciously, with a little extra thrown in. Yet another illusion shattered. Whatever his private life might be like, she had at least thought that his business was run on merit, not sex appeal.

'He's quite something, isn't he?' Donna said wistfully, patently wishing herself in Roberta's place, and quite unaware that her cousin had been working for Charles Lennox. Smoked salmon roulade was placed in front of her, and Donna's attention switched to her food. 'Oh, how good this looks!'

Lauren agreed without enthusiasm. Against her will, her eyes went to the window table again, in time to see Charles withdraw his hand to push back a rebel

swathe of dark hair. She felt stupidly pleased when his
hand was not returned to the table. Pleased, and then
angry to be pleased. How long-lasting this spell was
that he seemed to have cast over her. Determinedly
she picked up her knife and fork, and made conversation with Donna.

A few moments later Donna broke off what she was
saying to give a little wave. 'He's seen us. Aren't you
going to look, Lauren?'

'I'm enjoying my lunch far too much,' Lauren said,
studiously refusing to risk eye-contact with Charles
again. 'Who's in the Lodge, Donna?'

'No one,' her cousin said reluctantly. 'The agent
says the housing market's depressed.'

So all of this need never have happened, Lauren
thought. There weren't enough Charles Lennoxes
around to justify kicking me out of the Lodge. It could
be thought to serve Donna right.

Charles left shortly afterwards, and Lauren breathed
a sigh of relief though her eyes had clung hungrily to
his tall figure and dark head until the last moment
possible. Donna was going on at great length about
her new ideas for Allardyce House, most of the
monologue washing over Lauren and leaving no trace
in her mind. It must have been a quarter of an hour or
so later that the restaurant manager came over to tell
Lauren that she was wanted on the phone.

Puzzled, she followed him to the reception area. She
couldn't remember telling anyone where she was going
to be this lunchtime.

'What's going on?' Charles' voice asked tersely.

'You!' she said stupidly. 'Where are you?'

'At the office, of course,' he said impatiently. 'What
are you doing hobnobbing with that shrew of a cousin
of yours?'

'I beg your pardon?' Lauren exclaimed. 'That's my
business, just as your lunch appointments are yours.'

'You know what I'm getting at. Have you got a job yet?'

'Not yet. Look, Charles, I don't know what you're up to, but I'm in the middle of a social engagement. I must go.'

'Wait!' His tone was peremptory. 'Are you trying to get your old job back? Because if so, you're a bigger fool than I thought.'

'And you are insufferably rude! If you have nothing more important to say, I'll get back to my cousin.'

'Answer me, for God's sake!' he practically bellowed in her ear. 'If you are entertaining that crazy idea, let me tell you right now that it would be the biggest mistake of your life. Going back is deadly. It would be twice as bad as the original situation.'

'Charles,' she cut in calmly, touched in spite of herself that he appeared to care what happened to her, 'I am having lunch with my cousin. That's all. So far she doesn't even know that I need a job. But what I do is my business. It stopped being yours the instant I left your employment. And now I must go.'

'Are you going back home after lunch?' he asked peremptorily.

'Eventually, yes. I've a little shopping to do.'

'I must see you. Are you doing that wretched job tonight?'

'No. I'm doing two shifts tomorrow instead. But——'

'Six o'clock,' he cut in. 'You've got to be back by then.'

'We've nothing to say to each other,' she protested ineffectively.

'Speak for yourself.' The phone went dead.

'Who was it?' Donna asked when Lauren rejoined her.

'A colleague. Nothing important.'

'Good,' Donna said, only vaguely interested. 'I've

been thinking about Christmas. Have you made plans?'

'No. I've hardly thought about it.'

'Then you must come to me.' She smiled winningly across the table. 'Please, Lauren. For the family's sake. I haven't liked this rift. Your mother would want us to remain friends.'

'It's nice of you to ask me,' Lauren said, flabbergasted.

'So many family Christmases! Why not this year too?'

Well, why not? Lauren thought. This was obviously why Donna had fixed lunch. If her invitation were thrown back in her face, she would feel enormously hurt after making the first move. And for herself, something certain in the uncertain future would be good.

She smiled warmly. 'Thank you, Donna. It would be lovely to spend Christmas at Allardyce House.'

Donna's hands were clenched in tight fists against the white linen tablecloth, Lauren suddenly noticed. 'Brilliant!' her cousin said eagerly. 'Come early on Christmas Eve and stay until the morning after Boxing Day. I insist.'

'All right. It's a date.'

'Marvellous!' Only then did the plump fists uncurl, the fingers take up spoon and fork to attack the calorie-packed dessert. For a fleeting moment Lauren felt a tremor of unease. Was there more to this invitation than met the eye?

She banished the thought. It came from seeds sown by Charles Lennox's suspicious interrogation—and the food at Simonetto's was too delicious to spoil with unquiet thoughts.

The postman had delivered two items of mail after she set off for her lunch date. Lauren tore them open the moment she arrived home. Both were concerned with

money. One notified her of the council tax she would
be expected to pay. The other was from her landlord,
informing her that the exterior woodwork of the row
of cottages would be repainted early in the new year,
weather permitting. Lauren rented her cottage on a
full repairing lease, and the amount she would be
required to pay made her blink. Neither figure had
entered into her calculations on the subject of how far
her present money would go. The two debits would
cause serious trouble.

Her financial tangle weighing heavily on her mind,
she changed out of the smart suit she had worn for
lunch with Donna. She was wearing a favourite pair of
brown trousers and an amber sweater when she
opened the door to Charles' peremptory knock at six.

'Come in,' she said unenthusiastically.

He handed a tissue-wrapped bottle over. 'Something
to help the conversation along.'

She raised her eyebrows. '*That* kind of
conversation?'

'That depends on the turn it takes.'

'Very cryptic. I'll get glasses.'

When she came back from the kitchen he was
holding his hands towards the blazing logs, the warm
red glow colouring his face.

'So how did you survive your step back into the
past?' he asked.

'I had a pleasant lunch,' Lauren said calmly, handing
him the bottle and opener.

'Did she try anything on the job front?' He screwed
the bottle opener into the cork viciously and Lauren
had the feeling that he would have liked to puncture
Donna's plump body with it. The cork popped as he
withdrew it.

'Not a thing. But she did invite me to spend
Christmas at Allardyce House.'

'She's softening you up for something! What was
your answer?'

'I accepted.'

'Hmm.' He filled two glasses and handed one to her, touching it with his own. 'To a wary approach to all traps,' he said darkly.

'Oh, how ridiculous! To a delightful Christmas!' she said, rejecting his ominous toast.

'Now. . . Tell me what's been happening in this quite unnecessary job hunt of yours.' He leaned back in his chair, his glass loosely held, his apparent relaxation denied by the brooding concentration in the green eyes.

Lauren put a brave face on it. 'It's the wrong time of year to look for work. Everyone's thinking of Christmas and parties. I'm rapidly reconciling myself to the idea of not getting anything until after New Year. I'm sure something will turn up then.'

'How are you placed financially?'

'I'm fine,' she told him with clipped dismissiveness.

'Rubbish. You can't be.'

Lauren flushed. 'No doubt you mean well, Charles, but please don't continue in that vein. I can take care of myself.'

'As long as you get a free Christmas,' he said cynically.

'Oh, stop it!' Lauren said impatiently. 'I thought you had something important to discuss. Why not get round to it?'

'I'm in no particular hurry. That is the penalty you pay for creating relaxing environments.' He looked slowly round the lamplit room.

The silence lengthened until Lauren repeated, 'I wish you'd say what you've come to say.'

'How impatient you are.' He took another maddeningly slow sip of his wine, then put the glass down on the small table beside him. 'Very well, if you insist. I have a proposition to put to you, and an important rider to it. I'll begin with the proposition. You have no work, and you can't deny the fact that you need to earn money. I could put some work your way—and don't leap into a refusal before you know what I'm talking about.'

Lauren's mouth set in stubborn lines. Her brown eyes looked mutinously back at him. 'We've finished with that subject, Charles.'

'Hear me out. This is something entirely new. I have an empty house, just this week vacated by the builders who have been knocking it about for weeks. The place needs furnishing. You have a talent for that sort of thing. I would be happy and grateful if you could put that talent to work for me.'

Lauren was so staggered by the suggestion that she didn't immediately reject it. She remembered the empty rooms into which she had peered when she went to return Charles' pen, the gracious length of window and height of ceiling, the glimpse of attractive plasterwork and cornices. Her creative spirit leapt towards the task, but her mind rejected the thought of being offered what seemed like a kind of charity.

'A professional interior decorator is what you need,' she said.

'A professional job is just what I don't want,' he retorted emphatically. 'I don't want a bland straight-out-of-the-book look. I have family pieces that I want a home created around. I want someone with a love of places to be involved, not some whizz-kid earning a smart living from fabrics and carpet samples.'

'But I'm a complete amateur.'

'The word "amateur" is based on the Latin for "love". You love places. You transfer your love to them. I've seen three houses with your mark on them. I'm not trying to do you a favour. I'm asking you because it would be a privilege to have the sensitive care I've seen at Allardyce House, the Lodge, and here devoted to my own home.'

Lauren stared into the fire in silence for a moment, warning signals flashing in her mind. She had got away from this man reasonably unhurt. It was madness to contemplate coming back into his orbit. But there were the bills. . . Figures—red figures—replaced the warning lights. Could she afford to play safe?

Her eyes met his again, doubtfully. 'I would need to think.'

He nodded. 'Think as hard as you like. But let me give you a few financial details to put in the pot while you're doing so.'

'Don't even dream of being able to bribe me to do it,' Lauren said hotly, only to be ignored.

'The money is relevant. I have made enquiries. Advice from a professional would cost me a substantial sum.' He named a figure which caused Lauren's eyes to widen in shock. 'And remember that that would be for advice I most probably would not want. Advice from someone whose taste in furnishing I find sensitive and pleasing would be worth every penny as much, even more.'

Lauren shook her head proudly. 'If I accept your offer—if—I would agree to no more than my old salary for the length of time the work takes. Can we leave that subject now until I have had time to think hard about it?'

He shifted in his chair. 'Before you get down to serious thinking, you'd better listen to the rider. If the proposition gives you cause for so much thought, the rider will no doubt make you grind to a complete halt.' He looked broodingly at her. 'You may have noticed that I was not alone at Simonetto's.'

'Yes.' Lauren looked steadily back at him. 'You seemed to be. . .very much accompanied.'

'Too damned much!'

The look of annoyance on his face made amusement and something else suspiciously like pleasure bubble up inside her.

'That doesn't sound very civil,' she said demurely.

'I have been so civil that it hurts. Unfortunately,

more than mere civility is called for if the lady is to get
the message. Why the sceptical look? I'm serious about
this problem, you know.'

'I can see you're serious. Strange. . . I wouldn't
have put you down as the type to have problems with
a lady.'

He gave her a scathing look. 'It isn't as simple as
that. Believe me, if she were anyone else, she wouldn't
be a problem. But she represents one of the largest
contracts Spencer Travis has ever looked like landing.
Her firm has become part of a big conglomerate. If all
goes well and the lady remains interested, it could be
very big business indeed. The down side of all that is
that unfortunately I am being made increasingly aware
that I am expected to do rather more than land a
business deal.'

'Surely you only need to make the position clear?'

'And see my company lose a prime contract? Ever
heard of the venom of a woman scorned? You are a
complete innocent when it comes to business matters,
Lauren. One just does not make unpopular points
clear to a prospective client. One tries to get the
message across in some more subtle way—which is
what I have in mind.'

'Then I'm sure you'll do just that.' Her eyes were
cold. 'After all, I thought your track record was pretty
good when it comes to getting rid of unwanted
women.'

'I know you did,' he said icily. 'Leave that for the
moment. To get back to the point, what I need to
solve the present problem, is a personable, convincing
"other woman". I thought you would fit the bill
admirably.'

'You have a colossal cheek!' Lauren exploded.

'Not at all. As always, I have reason on my side.
You are convincingly attractive, and the fact that you
have moved away from my employment could be

interpreted as the result of our growing personal relationship.'

Lauren stared at him. 'You've thought it all out, haven't you? Well, count me out. The world's full of women.'

'If you were spending time at Longacre refurnishing my house,' he went on relentlessly, 'that would give further credibility.' His eyes challenged hers. 'But most important of all from my point of view, your opinion of involvement with bosses, ex-bosses and no doubt bosses-to-be, assures me that you'd not be likely to give me any trouble when it came to winding up the act—and believe me, I've had a cropfull of trouble along those lines.'

'So I've read—once again,' she said cuttingly. 'Do you really expect me, of all people, to help someone who has walked out on a girl in Imogen's position, as shown to the world in the latest tabloid dip into the murky waters of your private life?'

'I think,' he said crisply, 'that the time has come to put you right about the distorted image of me you've gathered from the newspapers. Yes, I've had a number of girlfriends. What normal man of my age hasn't? Farewells with each of them, until Imogen, were exchanged pleasantly, and with mutual consent.'

Lauren was looking at him, her brown eyes sceptical and condemning. She made no comment.

'Imogen, admittedly,' he went on, 'was different. I fell madly in love with her, madly being the operative word. She was incredibly beautiful and tremendously sexy, and I was beginning to feel it was time I settled down. But I see now that it was little more than infatuation that took me halfway to the altar with her.'

'And the prospect of children and responsibility that cut the journey short,' Lauren said, her voice tight with contempt.

He looked stonily at her. 'I pulled out because I

discovered the fact that Imogen was having another man's child.'

The silence was electric. 'Not yours?' Lauren said faintly. 'How do you know that?'

'Very easily. Imogen had daintily preserved herself for our wedding-night, largely, I fear, because my financial circumstances made it worth holding out for a wedding-ring. Unfortunately for her, her previous relationship had not been so circumspect. She deluded herself for some time about the pregnancy, but couldn't quite bring herself to go through with the wedding and take the consequences.'

Truth was in his eyes and his voice, not only in his words.

'Why on earth did you let the paper get away with blaming you for it?' Lauren asked slowly.

He shrugged. 'The stupid girl was in enough of a damned fix without my adding to it.'

Lauren swallowed. 'But the most recent photograph. Surely the implication of that was more than you should let them get away with?'

'The same governing factor for my silence applies—only more so. Imogen had counted on the child's father being persuaded to do the decent thing. In view of her behaviour, it's not altogether surprising that he wasn't eager to oblige. She apparently went on hoping until it was too late not to have the baby—not that she wanted to do that, in any case, or she'd have acted promptly and probably be Mrs Lennox by now. She apparently has massive debts, which made me such a desirable option in the first place. While I was in London she contacted me for help in sheer despair, and the bloody Press stumbled across us.'

'And *did* you help her? After what she'd done?' Lauren was having to reverse all her thinking about Charles. Before her bemused eyes the frog was turning into a prince, the beast into a paragon of virtue, and it was knocking her for six.

'There was still a baby to provide for, and parting with a bit of money, for someone with a thriving business like mine, is a very painless business,' he said dismissively. His clear, green gaze met her eyes directly. 'However, the whole affair leaves an unpleasant taste in the mouth. I hope you understand why I have, for the foreseeable future, had enough of women, and why seeking the help of someone as indifferent to the male sex as you are seems both desirable and sensible. Perhaps you'll bear that in mind when you consider your answer to what I'm asking of you.'

There was a silence.

'Do I take it that you feel you can't help out? You're as reluctant to give help as you are to accept it?' he said stiffly.

'I didn't say I wouldn't help,' she found herself protesting. 'You really are serious about both proposals?'

'Absolutely. This is big business, Lauren. I resent the need to ask for help, but the request is genuine.'

'I can't answer at once. I must think. You see that?'

'Of course. But on the Roberta matter, I can't wait indefinitely. I would like to know by tomorrow morning. If the answer's no, I would need to look else-where—and at the moment I must confess I haven't the faintest idea where. Certainly no one else has made it as clear as you have that I would be the last person on earth they would wish to become involved with.'

'I'll phone you with an answer to both questions first thing tomorrow morning,' Lauren told him, looking down at her clenching hands and avoiding his eyes.

'I hope to God it's yes.' He stood and picked up his jacket.

Lauren followed him over to the doorway, where he turned and she found herself close to him, looking up into his face.

'I don't want you to be under any misapprehension,' he said. 'If you do agree to help me to scare off Roberta on a personal level, you would have to put up with—and make—a show of affection. It wouldn't achieve anything if you shrank away from being touched and looked as though you couldn't bear the thought of being kissed. It would of course be play-acting, done always with the targeted audience in mind. But you'll need to know that you can cope.'

Lauren swallowed hard. 'I'll think about that, too,' she said.

'Good.' A brief smile played round his lips. 'I think all the cards are on the table now. I'll leave you to study your hand. Goodnight, Lauren.'

'Goodnight,' she said breathlessly.

When she had closed the door she went and sat by the fire. What he had told her seemed to have shifted the balance of everything, both between the two of them and in herself as an individual. An incredible jumble of emotions was in turmoil inside her. One by one, she drew them to the surface of her mind and considered them.

Charles first. Her whole idea of the kind of man he was had to be reformed. Instead of the irresponsible predator she had thought him, he now appeared to be the victim of a scheming woman. Lauren marvelled at the strength with which he had triumphed over the situation, not seeking revenge, keeping silent out of sheer gallantry, and, amazingly, even helping the woman who had tried so despicably to deceive him.

No wonder that in her heart of hearts it had never been easy for Lauren to think ill of him. Her eyes stung with tears. It was as though his care for the baby who was no concern of his somehow weighed against her own father's callousness and began to wash the bitterness of it out of her. For that, she ought to be prepared to do anything for him.

But could she do what he asked? There was no

need, now, to deny and fight against the fact that she
loved him. And yet there was every need, for hadn't
he told her clearly that the only reason he turned to
her was her determined resistance to him? Instead of
a woman who didn't trust men, there was a man who
had good reason not to trust women. Could she act
the part of his girlfriend, with all the emotional, loving
outward show he had told her would be necessary,
without betraying the fact that the outward show was
the only too true reflection of what she really felt?

Throughout the night she was torn between desire
to help him and fear of failing to hide her feelings. But
in the cold light of dawn she was left with two
overwhelmingly persuasive facts. Charles needed help.
How could she refuse this chance to make reparation
for all the ill she had thought of him? And she couldn't
live on air. How could she turn down what was
probably her only chance to avoid deep financial
trouble over the dead Christmas and New Year
period? Life couldn't be lived on the basis of what was
desirable, what was easy. She had no real choice in
this matter.

At the promised time, she phoned to tell Charles
that she would do what he asked, hoping desperately
that she could do it with dignity.

Roberta's business trip abroad gave a few days for
Lauren to try to adjust to her new status. Early on the
foloowing Sunday afternoon, she was receiving her first
briefing in the Longacre service flat before a visit from
Roberta to discuss—Charles had told Lauren with a
sceptical smile—one or two points in the proposed
contract.

'I don't want us to aim at anything heavy,' he
stressed. 'I want her to wonder why you're here, not
have the reason rammed down her throat. If she goes
away undecided whether it's work or play that has
brought us together, that will be just about right. I

suggest we make some mention of your involvement in plans for Longacre. She can find us having coffee after what might have been a working lunch—and wonder whether it was just that, or otherwise.'

'Right. I'll get the props organised.' Lauren perched on the corner of the settee near the coffee-pot, and began to fill two cups.

The sounds of a car scattering gravel prevented further preparation. Charles gave her shoulder a quick, encouraging squeeze, and went down the out-side staircase, while Lauren hastily reached for a Sunday colour supplement, feeling incredibly nervous. Could she possibly look like the sort of woman Charles Lennox might take a second look at? Was the skirt of her Italian knitted suit too short, its soft rose colour too obviously feminine? Could she ever pull this mad pretence off?

There was the sound of voices coming back up the staircase and Charles ushered Roberta through the doorway.

'Come in, come in. You two have met before, haven't you?' he said pleasantly.

There was a momentary flicker in Roberta's blue eyes. Then she was smiling, though the smile didn't reach her eyes, and saying, 'Yes. Laura, isn't it? You work for Charles.'

The eyes and the 'Laura' were effective. Lauren put aside the colour supplement, and coolly crossed her legs. 'Lauren, actually,' she said. 'We did meet briefly when I was working for Charles.'

'You should have told me you had another engage-ment today,' Roberta said, turning to Charles with a reproachful sweep of her long lashes. 'I don't want to interrupt with my boring old business.'

Charles gave her a reassuring smile. 'Business is never boring. I'm entirely at your disposal. Lauren can amuse herself for a while, I'm sure.'

'Or I can leave if you prefer it? I don't mind. We

can always talk another time,' Lauren offered
pleasantly.

'Not unless you're in a desperate hurry. I'd still like
to go round the house with you today.' He turned to
Roberta. 'Lauren is going to give me expert advice on
the Longacre décor.'

Roberta looked with unflattering surprise at Lauren.
'Really? That's quite a change of direction for you,
isn't it?'

'Yes, it is, rather,' Lauren said, smiling sweetly.
'One I'm apparently thought capable of taking,
though.' She turned to Charles. 'If you're sure you
want me to stay on, I'll make myself useful with the
lunch dishes. And perhaps Roberta would like tea? I
think our coffee will be cold by now.'

'Can you spare the time?' he asked Roberta with
charming solicititude. 'I know how valuable a com-
modity free days are in your busy life.' His tone
seemed to convey both admiration and care. Lauren
blinked as she admired his acting ability.

'That would be rather nice,' Roberta said charmingly, but the cold light in her eyes as she directed a
smile of assent in Lauren's direction showed that she
had notched up the reference to lunch.

'Then in that case, thank you, Lauren,' Charles said.
'You know where everything is, don't you?'

'No problem.'

Lauren closed the door behind herself with a sigh of
relief. So far, so good, she thought. Certain seeds had
been sown in Roberta's mind. Now they needed time
to develop.

They were still deep in conversation when she took
the tea-tray in and poured three cups. Taking her own
and the colour magazine to a seat by the window, she
sat quietly pretending to read but in reality feasting
her eyes on Charles until she realised what she was
doing and determinedly raised the colour supplement
to cut off her view of him.

It was Roberta who rose at last, and with a charming glance at Lauren, said, 'I really mustn't hold you two back from work for a moment longer. It's good of you to have given me so much time, Charles. And I do hope it hasn't been too boring for you, Lauren.'

'Not at all.' She gave a contented kitten stretch. 'Reading the papers and drinking tea on Sunday afternoon is no hardship.'

'And at least you've had a little woman to do the dishes for you, you lucky man!' Roberta told Charles.

Cow! Lauren thought ferociously, free to wipe the pleasant smile off her face as Charles escorted out to the car the woman who had just succeeded in reducing her to the status of kitchen-maid.

He grinned as he came back into the flat. 'The knives are out, I believe.'

'How did we do?' she asked.

'Pretty well. I imagine we gave Roberta one or two things to think about. But something's occurred to me.'

'What's that?'

'I think we need to do a bit of quiet rehearsing.'

'Rehearsing?'

'So that when the need arises, we know we can kiss convincingly.'

Lauren's heart lurched. 'You're joking!'

He looked steadily at her. 'Why should you think that? I told you this was a serious business.'

'But I've already accepted that it might be necessary,' she said, avoiding his eyes.

'It won't be for the first time, though, will it? And previous experiences both sprang from and caused bad feeling. We need to be sure we can forget those times and kiss with apparent pleasure and the confidence of familiarity. Like this, perhaps. . .'

She found herself gathered close in strong male arms, and looked up in alarm, her heart beating like a

wild thing, only to have any protest silenced as his
mouth closed gently on hers.

She closed her eyes, helplessly melting against him
at first. Not like this, her mind protested, struggling
against her racing blood and quickening breath. Fear
of discovery made her freeze in his arms.

He paused, withdrawing his lips from hers and
looking down into her face, a questioning look in his
eyes. 'Yes, I was right,' he said thoughtfully. 'You're
tense. Too rigid by far. Put your arms round my
neck. . . No, closer than that. Remember you're the
girl I love. We take infinite pleasure in this—or so
people must think. Now, try again.'

Again his mouth closed on hers. Lauren's eyes
closed in blind panic against the dazzling clarity of his
green gaze, assessing her performance at such close
quarters. Again primitive emotion raced through her.
You can't do this, her nerves cried out.

When he broke away this time, she was breathing
rapidly.

'Better?' she whispered desperately, hoping her
voice didn't sound as choked to his ears as it did to her
own.

'Much. But remember, lovers are always reluctant
to separate. Don't pull away so abruptly next time.
Imagine that there's nothing you'd like more than to
stay in my arms for ever. One more try?'

This time Lauren was lost—completely. Before she
could close them, she felt her eyes cloud with passion
as he drew her towards him again. Her body moulded
itself to his with melting ease. Her arms were not
content with meekly going round his neck. Her hands
took on life of their own, greedily pulling him closer,
her fingers feverishly exploring the springy hair curling
in the nape of his neck, the softness of the skin behind
his ears.

She heard nothing. It was Charles who raised his
head suddenly. Lauren opened her eyes with an invol-

untary murmur of protest and saw him looking over her shoulder, obviously focusing on something else.

'Roberta!' he said quite calmly, gently releasing Lauren. 'Is something wrong with the car?'

Lauren, her lips swollen, her eyes languorous, stood there with crimson face, consumed with embarrassment.

Roberta stepped coolly towards the settee and stooped to pick up a file.

'The car's fine. I stupidly forgot this. So sorry to have disturbed you again.' Her eyes flickered to Lauren's lowered face, then back to Charles, but her self-possession was admirable. 'This time I really am on my way.'

Protesting urbanely at the idea of intrusion, Charles once again walked out with her.

When he came back, Lauren was sufficiently in control of herself to say, 'So much for the subtle approach. She can't have been left in much doubt about that.'

He gave a brief smile. 'I was right, then. You didn't hear the car stop round the front of the house?'

Lauren looked at him, suddenly realising the implication of that. 'You knew she was coming?'

'I knew she'd be back. It was on the cards that she'd want to know what was going on after she left. And she left the file. I'd seen that. Roberta doesn't forget anything. It was obviously left behind with intention.'

She didn't want to believe her ears. 'All that was done on purpose? You wanted her to find you kissing me? Doesn't that go against everything you were saying about keeping it light?'

He shrugged. 'If people try to take you by surprise, then they might as well find what they are expecting to find.'

'You could at least have warned me.'

'If you'd been expecting it, you wouldn't have

reacted in quite the same genuinely embarrassed way. Well, would you?'

'Maybe not.' Lauren stared down at the floor, fighting to control her feelings. The urge to escape was overwhelming. The force-field between her and Charles was so strong. How could he not be aware of it? With an effort she picked up her bag. 'If you want to go over Longacre, we'd better get on with it,' she said stiffly.

He shook his head dismissively. 'That can wait until after Christmas. Operation Roberta has first priority.'

'In that case,' she said, limp with relief, 'since I take if that Operation Roberta is over for today, I'll be on my way.'

'Just one more thing before you go. We haven't talked money. I still think you're worth more, but I respect your wishes, and I shall be paying you your old salary as from the point of agreement last Saturday,' he said.

The contrast between his talk of money and the painful, real feelings he had aroused in her seemed like the last straw.

'Thank you. That's fine,' she said, her voice clipped. 'I'll be off, then.'

She almost ran across the room, then down the steps and round to her car.

Acting, she thought as she drove blindly home. That was all he was doing. That was what she had to remember. Acting for Roberta, acting for her. Roberta too, who couldn't have been delighted by what she had seen, had managed to cover up any frustration she felt like an old pro.

But what about Lauren Frazer? she thought bitterly. She had been the member of the cast to come closest to ruining the production, totally incapable of preventing Charles' pseudo-passion from arousing an all too genuine reaction in herself.

She was going to have to do better than that. She

148 FREE TO LOVE

gripped the steering-wheel in desperate frustration.
She had known it was going to be difficult, but this
afternoon had convinced her what torture was in store
as she tried to live through the coming weeks without
betraying herself.

CHAPTER NINE

LAUREN, curled in the corner of her sofa, stared hungrily at Charles' handsome face on the television screen. He was being interviewed by the local network, and for once she could watch him with unveiled eyes and uncontrolled expression. She fiercely resented each brief cut to the interviewer, aching only to feast her gaze on the perfect bone-structure of the face she loved and stare unchecked into the brilliance of the eyes that so bewitched her.

These days, it was only when she was supposed to be acting the part of a girl in love that she was true to herself, she thought. How paradoxical her behaviour was. When she was alone with Charles, a performance uncalled for, that was when the acting began: the false indifference, the pseudo-unawareness of his every move and thought. It would have been so easy and so natural, when they were alone, to look and touch as she was only allowed to do in public.

Charles sensed her tension, she felt. Perhaps he expected their association to make them more relaxed with each other, easy in private as they managed to be in public. He didn't question her, but she was conscious of his eyes watching and wondering.

Perhaps it wouldn't be for much longer. Roberta seemed to be getting the message as painlessly as Charles had wished, and it looked at though the contract would be signed early in the New Year.

The interview was being wound up now, Charles smiling in acknowledgement of the presenter's thanks against a panning shot of Longacre, then the studio linkman appeared on screen again. Lauren reached out and switched off the set.

She was growing to love Longacre. As she worked on it, the house stole into her heart and demanded to be taken seriously and fill her mind when nothing else managed to oust thoughts of Charles.

He was going to Norfolk for Christmas, where he had grown up and where his mother still lived in the family home. Christmas in Norfolk, apparently, was very special. Tonight, the night before Christmas Eve, was the last time Lauren would see him before the holiday began. Would being away from him bring relief or pain?

'Running late, I'm afraid,' he told her as they drove back to Longacre after he had picked her up. 'I've not tagged my Christmas parcels. Can't cope with those fiddly little strings. Could you fix them for me while I finish organising the drinks?'

'Of course,' Lauren told him, the mention of Christmas presents making her uneasy. She had agonised long and hard on the subject. As Charles' apparent girlfriend, she felt she should give him something. As his employee, she felt she shouldn't. As her real self, she had longed to choose a gift for him. In the end she had decided to forget the subject.

The parcels were spread out on his bed, each tag placed neatly on the appropriate one. Gifts for his mother, aunts and uncles, someone called Buffy—maybe his mother's housekeeper, she decided. Then she came to a gold-wrapped, silver-ribboned package, slender and oblong—a jeweller's box?—and its gift tag shattered her world.

'To darling Danielle, love and a million happy memories, Charles-next-door'.

The scenario was plain, the reason Norfolk was special obvious. A lifetime of growing affection and familiarity seemed to lie behind the words. What lay ahead of them?

Lauren pictured the girl next door, a girl who shone like a timeless star against the tawdry glitter of the

ephemeral women who had come after her. A girl
whom he was now beginning to see in a different light?
Loving familiarity poised to grow into love?

The spectre of the unknown Danielle seemed to
hover over that last evening.

'Are you all right?' Charles asked as he stopped the
car in Cherwell Terrace. 'You've been rather quiet
tonight.'

'Afraid of putting a foot wrong before so many of
your friends, I expect,' she said.

He twisted round in the driving seat so that he could
look down at her. 'I thought we were getting to be old
hands at the game.'

'That's just when you can slip up dreadfully.'

His eyes scanned her face, coming back to meet her
own, his mouth twisting with rueful amusement. 'You
take life so damned seriously, don't you?'

'Not entirely. I take my *work* seriously.'

'And tonight was work.' He sighed impatiently. 'I
wish I could be convinced that you were at least going
to have a little fun over Christmas.' He reached over
into the back and brought over a Christmas parcel
which he dropped into her lap. 'This is for you.'

Dismay flooded through Lauren. 'Oh! I haven't got
anything for you. I didn't know if I should or not. . .'

He put his fingers to her lips, silencing her anguished
protest. 'Hush! Aren't you giving me enough with all
this serious work you keep doing?'

His hand trailed slowly over her cheek, then down
to cup her chin. He lowered his head and kissed her
on the lips, as it had been decided they should do on
meeting and parting in public. 'Happy Christmas,
Lauren,' he said softly. The words too caressed her
lips as he spoke them.

'Happy Christmas.' Her eyes, staring longingly into
his, were filling with stupid tears. She looked away
hastily and fumbled with the door. 'Thank you for my
present. Please don't get out.' She managed to let

herself into the house before bursting into tears, hugging the book—for it obviously was a book—to her breast as though it would ease the pain she felt.

In a little while she unwrapped the parcel, because she couldn't take it to Allardyce House. It was an illustrated history of English furniture, the sort of book she would never afford to buy for herself, and which would give her immense pleasure. It had been thoughtfully chosen, but safely too. Who could read romance into a history of furniture? And the gift tag said simply 'To Lauren, with my gratitude, Charles'. No past, no future for her. She belonged only to the present. But in Norfolk a girl wreathed in a million happy memories was waiting to welcome him home for Christmas.

She didn't hear from him until the early afternoon of New Year's Eve, when his voice caught her unawares over the telephone, making her feel as though the blood had drained from her face and sped to her heart, swelling it so hugely that it ached to hear him.

'Lauren? How did it go?'

The ability to be quite honest about her Christmas saved her. 'I'll say "I told you so" for you before I answer that.'

'So there *was* an ulterior motive?' he said triumphantly.

'A dozen of them. Donna had launched a "Christmas at Allardyce House" scheme, and found once she had taken the bookings that she couldn't get the necessary extra staff required to cope with twelve guests. I was unsuspecting free help scheduled to fetch and carry and call it Christmas *en famille*,' she told him drily.

'You didn't let her get away with it?' he said, outraged.

'Not at all. I sat down and negotiated a nice fat working-Christmas salary for myself.'

Laughter exploded down the line. 'Good for you. The docile little worm has learned how to turn, at last. I bet that shook her.'

'It did, rather. But we remained on more or less friendly terms. How was Christmas in Norfolk?'

'Delightful, as always. I was well cosseted and fussed over. All highly satisfying. But life can't be all tinsel and fairy-lights, can it? more's the pity.' A regretful sigh. 'I must come down to earth again. Are you all set for tonight?'

'Of course,' Lauren said, subdued. No mistaking which side of the magic she was stacked.

'New Year has its magic too,' he said. An after-thought, but it made her heart soar again. 'I'll pick you up at eight, then.'

Lauren checked herself in front of the mirror, almost feverish at the thought of seeing him again. Against the black velvet of her dress and lace jacket there was a flush of delicate colour in her creamy skin. She fixed the Victorian chandelier earrings Donna had given her. Her dark eyes, dancing with excitement, seemed to match their sparkle.

Her heart leapt at the sound of the doorbell, and she fought down her dangerously volatile feelings as she went to the door.

Charles was almost unbearably handsome in his dinner-jacket and snowy shirt. Her eyes devoured him, and she couldn't stop her lips curving into the most delighted of smiles at the sight of him.

'You look absolutely lovely,' he said as he handed her a creamy orchid in a transparent box.

'You too. Good, I mean.' She realised that she was staring goofily at him and lowered her eyes to the corsage he had given her. 'Thank you, Charles. This is beautiful.' She fumbled with box, flower and pin, dropping the latter. Charles stopped to pick it up.

'Let me,' he said calmly.

Lauren didn't know how she bore the touch of his fingers against her breast as he fixed the orchid in place on the flimsy lace of the jacket. Her flesh seemed to fire with awareness of him. When he reached for her red velvet wrap and put it round her, it felt like an embrace. She was mad, she told herself, but the feeling of being on a high refused to die down.

Her face rested against his as they danced, his arm pulling her close against his body, not two people but one, it seemed, as they danced in a relaxed silence of mental and physical harmony.

As they headed for the supper-room in the interval, Charles' arm was still lightly around her waist, and he dropped a kiss on to the top of her head.

'Aren't we putting on a performance for no reason?' Lauren asked, overcome by guilt at the pleasure this gave her. Roberta, who should have been there, was unexpectedly abroad on business.

'Still plenty of Roberta's spies around. Besides. . .' He paused, and Lauren looked up at him.

The green eyes looked with teasing challenge into hers. 'It's becoming rather a habit.' She blushed, and he squeezed her hard, laughing at her as he swept her into the supper-room.

It seemed all one with the magic of the evening when one of the raffle tickets he had bought her was first out of the drum. To Lauren's utter astonishment, she had won not just any old prize, but the star prize of the evening, a fortnight's holiday for two in a private villa on Grenada, to be taken in January.

'Grenada! I don't believe this!' she said as Charles gave her a gentle push forward. He seemed inordinately amused by her luck.

'You must have the prize, of course,' she said awkwardly when she came back from accepting the travel agent's voucher. 'You gave me the tickets. No way could I consider the holiday mine. In any case, it's a job for one I need, not a holiday for two.' She had a

momentary painful picture of Danielle beside him in a
sunny paradise.

'Don't be so ridiculous! I know Grenada like the
back of my hand. I can have as many holidays as I like
there whenever I want. Never look a gift horse in the
mouth, you silly girl,' he told her calmly, closing her
hand firmly round the voucher. 'If no work turns up,
you are at least sure of two cost-free weeks. Someone
up there must be looking after you.'

He had spoken so calmly of the time after her
association with him ended, and a Cinderella-like
feeling enveloped Lauren as midnight approached.
The usual relayed chimes of Big Ben echoed in her
heart with notes of doom. She felt to have no part in
the ritual singing of 'Auld Lang Syne' and light-hearted
exchange of kisses between all and sundry. Charles'
kiss was haunted by a feeling of finality.

'Let's get a breath of air,' he said as the band struck
up again, steering her in the direction of the
conservatory.

It was quiet and cool in there, and they walked
along the leafy paths in silence, meeting no one.
Lauren was thankful for the subdued lighting. The
birth of the New Year had been unbearably poignant.
Where would she be at the next New Year's beginning? Where would Charles be? One thing was certain.
They wouldn't be greeting it together.

'All that frantic fun and merriment,' Charles said
suddenly, cutting into her thoughts. They had stopped
in the shadow of a citrus tree in the orangery, and the
scent of the fruit was piquant in the air, unnaturally
ripe in this unfruitful season. 'Am I the only one in the
world to feel that underneath it all there's a great big
question mark, almost a sense of menace?'

She turned, startled that his feelings mirrored her
own. 'You feel that too?'

His green eyes looked deeply into hers. 'Tonight I
do.' He reached out for her hands, and cradled both

of them in his. 'Let's forget the froth and frolic. We've got an infant year here in our hands. Tell me honestly what you hope it will bring.'

For a wild moment as their eyes locked, she considered answering him as he asked, honestly. What if she told him that she hoped desperately that he would stop seeing her as a useful actress to help him out of an embarrassing situation? What if she told him how much she wished 'Darling Danielle' had never been born, and that Norfolk held no attractions to compare with those he was looking at this very moment?

There was a strange intensity in his eyes. 'Come on,' he said urgently, giving her hands an admonishing shake. 'There must be something you long for?'

She swallowed the madness. 'Can't you guess? A job!'

The build-up of intensity in the air around them came crashing down. His face changed. Anger replaced the questioning light in his eyes, and his grip tightened crushingly.

'Is that the best you can come up with? A bloody job? What about that gaping, empty life of yours? Don't you ever in a wild moment contemplate allowing someone into it? Have you the least idea what it would be like to love someone? Or isn't such a thought permitted to enter that ice-cold desert of a brain of yours?'

Lauren looked down at their hands, refusing to meet his eyes, afraid of what he would read in hers. 'Let me go, Charles.'

'Have you ever loved anyone?' he asked her fiercely.

'Of course. Lot of people.' She could feel the blood draining from her face. She had brought this on herself, with all her dangerous excitement. She was bringing them both close to the edge of disaster.

'I'm not talking about "lots of people" love. I'm talking about "man and woman" love.' His voice was contemptuous. 'Where *are* the men in your life? Have you any normal feelings? You deserve to be shocked into discovering them. For two pins I'd do it!'

There were voices and laughter from the other end of the conservatory. If someone hadn't walked in at that moment, heaven only knew what would have happened.

The crazy light in his eyes died down, his fingers relaxed their painful grip and his arms dropped to his sides as he almost threw her hands away. Lauren shrank away from him. 'I'd like to go home now,' she said with difficulty. 'I've done my duty for tonight. This is way beyond it.'

'Afraid of a man laying a hand on you?' His voice was low but venomous. 'Afraid that you might conceivably feel something?'

'No,' she said with shaky dignity. 'I'm afraid that you will say or do something you will be sorry about when you come to your senses. Please take me home.'

They drove along the deserted roads in silence—oh, such a different silence now—the headlamps cutting a swathe through the darkness, trees, darkened houses, the occasional glowing window appearing and falling behind like a fast-moving film.

He pulled up in front of Cherwell Terrace and silently waited for her to get out.

Lauren tried desperately to make their next meeting easier.

'I've got all the plans for Longacre worked out now. Will you go through them as soon as possible so that the work can begin?'

'Oh, well, *business*. . .' he said, with excessive emphasis on the word. 'I expect we can wax eloquent on the subject of *business*, don't you? Come over in time for a working coffee tomorrow and we'll talk nice, safe facts and figures. You'll cope with that, I expect.'

'It's obvious that you would have preferred to be somewhere else and with someone else on New Year's

Eve,' she said brokenly, and turned to run and put the shelter of her own front door between them.

If only he knew how little she needed to be encouraged to give rein to her emotions. It would have been the greatest indulgence and relief to fling herself into his arms and cry that *he* was what she wanted more than anything, her only real desire, a desire that tormented her with a pain that was more exquisite than anything she had ever experienced. But how his irritation at her imagined coldness would have changed to embarrassed revulsion then.

She blamed herself as much as him. A combination of his own wish to be spending New Year's Eve with Danielle, and her own uncontrolled sexuality had brought about this evening's disaster.

She shivered with fear and doubts of her own ability to see through the cruel farce they were playing out. The furnishing of Longacre just had to be completed as quickly as possible. Only then would she escape from this painful charade of a relationship.

Dressed for courage in brown tracksuit pants and a bright red sweater for her appointment at Longacre, Lauren pulled a red bobble hat over her dark curls and well down to cover her ears. It was bitterly cold and it had snowed in the night, but not enough to make the short journey tricky. She wondered nervously what kind of atmosphere would exist between herself and Charles after the night before, and viewed the day with apprehension.

But a more familiar, mannerly Charles in comfortable fawn cords and a heavy Norwegian sweater met her at the door of the flat.

'You look like a robin in the snow. Come in,' he said calmly.

'With an *en suite* red nose!' Lauren retorted, finding it a relief to be greeted with something like humour.

'My apologies for last night,' he said once the door was closed, turning to look at her. 'You were right. I *was* wishing things were different. But I shouldn't have taken my vexation out on you.'

'That's all right.' She pretended to be deeply interested in the contents of her document case.

'No, it's not.' He took the case from her and put it on the floor. 'I was insufferably rude. At least let me apologise for it.'

She shrugged. 'Better me than someone who matters.'

He frowned. 'What makes you speak as though *you* don't matter? Why diminish yourself in that stupid way?'

Go on in this vein, and they would be heading for trouble again. With no one to defuse the atmosphere, that was the last thing she wanted to happen.

'I meant mattered in a business sense. But please— do let's forget it. I almost had before I got here. I completely have after that very civil apology.' She waved her papers at him. 'Look. Lots of plans for you to think about.'

He smiled, a warm, crooked, half-rueful smile that turned an invisible knife in her heart as he removed the bobble hat by its pom-pom and threw it on a chair. 'You have a forgiving nature, Lauren. And all I can offer by way of a reward is coffee. But it's ready and hot. I'll bring it through. Spread that stack of papers of yours out on the table, then we can go through them comfortably.'

Lauren felt almost light-headed with relief as Charles disappeared into the kitchen. Jeeves, wanting his own share of attention, leapt up on the windowsill at her side and sent a silver photograph frame crashing to the floor.

'Oh, Jeeves! That was rather silly, wasn't it?' She stooped to pick up the photograph. It was new since Christmas, a striking outdoor portrait of a fresh and sunny-looking girl, with shining blue eyes and fair hair blown back from her laughing face.

This is her, Lauren thought, a sudden pain constricting her breathing. She was looking at Danielle, the Danielle whom she would have liked to hate. Instead, looking down at the picture in her hands, it was only too easy to understand why such a girl should be not just Danielle, but darling Danielle. And why Charles should regret exchanging Christmas with such a happy, radiant creature for someone whose eyes and hair were dark as night, who was scared rigid by her love for him, and who looked like nothing more exotic than a robin.

Charles came in and she started guiltily.

'Jeeves was peeved because I hadn't spoken to him,' she said. 'He knocked this off in his attempt to hog my attention.'

He took the frame from her and looked down at it with a reminiscent smile. 'A Christmas present. I grew up next door to Danielle. She's as lovely as she looks. Strange how you overlook the treasures near at hand, don't you think?' He put the photograph carefully back in its place, his eyes reluctant to leave it, and scowled at Jeeves. 'No more of that, you furry fathead.'

Jeeves walked off into the kitchen in high dudgeon and Charles, with an air of wanting to get on with business, invited Lauren to begin discussing her plans for the big house.

An hour or so later, everything had gone through on the nod.

'I knew you would be on my wavelength,' Charles said. 'I couldn't have spelled out what I wanted for Longacre—only what I didn't want. You seem to have got it exactly right. Now it's a question of waiting for tradespeople to be available, I suppose?'

'Well, no, actually. I've got them on standby. It's not a busy time of year,' she told him. 'The decorators can move in tomorrow. The furnishing fabrics and curtain materials are all available without delay. All I need is the go-ahead from you.'

'Then you've got it.' He looked at his watch. 'About time I took you off to lunch, I think.'

'Oh, please—no. Unless it's for the Roberta business.'

He looked coolly at her. 'It just might be possible that I want to take you to lunch for other reasons——'

'I've eaten so much over the holiday that I'd prefer to do without. Truly!' she interrupted nervously.

'—one of the most important being to ensure that last night is fully forgiven,' he went on as though she hadn't spoken.

'Of course it is,' she said, gathering up her papers.

'But if you swan off home I shall think you're still sulking.'

'Well, I'm not,' she said emphatically.

'If we go and eat, you can prove it.'

She looked at him, running out of opposition. 'You are a most insistent man.'

'So I'm told,' he said calmly. 'If you've any sense at all you'll save yourself both time and effort. We are eating out.' He plonked her bobble hat over one of her eyes and swept her down the steps and into his car.

At least things weren't horrible between them any more, Lauren thought as they drove through the pristine white lanes. The world seemed very beautiful, with Charles' hand on the gear lever, his broad shoulder almost touching her, the faint, spicy, masculine smell of his cologne in the air. She closed her eyes against the brief, transitory spell of it all. She was glad the unpleasantness had subsided, but oh, to be Danielle, the 'treasure near at hand', who had a lifetime of moments such as this ahead of her.

Work at Longacre continued with crises and solutions following each other in quick succession. Charles and

Lauren were never alone together at the house now, and the presence of workmen made things easier.

The contract between Spencer Travis and Roberta's company was duly signed, but Charles insisted that a gradual tailing off not a sudden ending of his make-believe relationship with Lauren was necessary, so there was still the odd social occasion to cope with.

There were times when Charles was away, whether in Norfolk or on business Lauren never knew. Then she tortured herself by imagining the laughing face of the photograph looking adoringly up into his, while she laboured over the furnishing of the house where she supposed it was inevitable that Charles and Danielle would live one day.

The photograph in its heavy silver frame was constantly moved around from one position to another in the service flat. Sometimes it was over the fireplace, sometimes on the table near his chair. It was as though he couldn't bear to be far from it, wherever he was. Once it was nowhere in sight, and Lauren knew that it was in Charles' bedroom. She came close to opening the door and proving her suspicions, but she stopped short of an action that would have made her both ashamed and miserable. The fact of Danielle was there, there was no denying it. Why torture herself by seeking visible proof of it?

By the middle of the third week in January, work on Longacre was almost completed, and Lauren, exhausted by the strain of being physically near Charles and yet in every way that mattered a million miles away from him, was longing for her task to be over. She had got up on Wednesday morning feeling out of sorts, and was sorely tempted to go back to bed, but deliveries were expected at the house.

She battled all day against the growing certainty that she was really cooking up an illness, not just vaguely unwell, as her body ranged from uncontrollable shivering to profuse sweating, while her aching head

pounded, Give in! Give in! She was hanging curtains
at an upstairs window when she saw a car draw up at
the front of the house. The thought of having to speak
to someone was daunting. She had not yet put the
lights on, and she shrank back into the shelter of the
curtains, determined to ignore the bell and let whoever
had turned up obey the instructions on the front door
and try the flat behind the house, where Charles was
working at home.

Two women got out, the younger of the two helping
the older woman and solicitously turning up the collar
of her fur coat against the cold wind. It was when the
younger woman turned round that Lauren saw the
vivid blue of her eyes, the dazzling blonde hair under
the black fur hat, and realised that she was looking at
Danielle. The older woman she guessed to be Charles'
mother. It was obvious from their attitude towards
each other—the matter-of-course taking of Danielle's
arm, the affectionate way Danielle looked down at the
older woman and spoke to her—that there was a warm
and easy relationship between them.

Charles had said nothing about their coming. The
fact that Danielle could turn up unexpectedly was
further indication of the close relationship between
them.

A fierce pain stabbed through Lauren's chest, not
attributable to whatever bugs were invading her
system. She watched the two women disappear round
the corner of the house, and imagined every detail of
Charles' welcome: the look in his eyes when he opened
the door and saw Danielle's radiant face, the delighted
kiss and hug he would give her, the treasure it had
taken him so long to discover.

He would bring them to look over Longacre, of
course. Lauren filled with panic and despair. He would
introduce her to both of them. She couldn't bear it.
Even if she had been well, it would have been an
ordeal. Feeling as she did, it was impossible.

She finished hanging the last curtain with scant attention to the evenness of its folds, then grabbed her coat and let herself out by the front door to drive herself home. She was running away, but there were times when it was the only possible thing to do.

At home she filled a hot-water bottle, dropped her clothes on the bedroom floor, and sank into bed, shivering, sick and miserable. She must have fallen asleep at once, because it was dark when she was roused by a voice—Charles' voice, she suddenly realised. 'Go away!' she croaked, but he didn't hear, because his voice was nearer now, calling, 'I'm coming up.'

'Anyone could have walked in. You hadn't locked the door. Why did you leave Longacre without saying anything?' he said from the bedroom doorway.

'I'm ill,' she protested feebly. The light was switched on, hurting her eyes. 'Put it off,' she begged.

He looked hard at her, then did as she asked and walked over to the bed to light the much more gentle Tiffany lamp.

Then he stood looking down at her again. She flounced over, turning tetchily away from him. A cool hand was placed on her head.

'Burning up, aren't you?' he said. 'Well, it's not difficult to diagnose what's wrong with you. You're a late flu victim. I thought you looked as though you were heading for it when you insisted all was well this morning. Had any medication?'

'No. Stop looking at me!' she said childishly.

'You look damned rough.'

'That's because you've come straight from Danielle.' She caught his eye, and the tail end of a knowing smile. 'Yes, I saw them arrive. She—she's very beautiful.'

'No need to turn green. So are you—on a good day!'

'I don't have good days,' she said dispiritedly, reaching for a tissue.

'That's the flu talking. We'd better do something about it. Got anything? Aspirins? Beecham's powders?'

'Bathroom.' Speaking was both painful and a super-human effort.

He disappeared and came back with a glass of water and a couple of pills which hurt like hell as she swallowed them.

'Are you warm?' he asked.

'Sometimes. Up and down. At the moment I'm freezing.'

'Got a hot-water bottle?'

'It's gone cold.'

He felt under the duvet, and encountered her icy feet. His hand lingered on them, warm and, even in her present state, sensual.

'Ten arctic toes here. We'll soon change that.'

He found the bottle and took it away downstairs. The touch of his hand had made Lauren crumble. She sniffled unhappily into the pillow until he came back.

He smiled down at her as he gave her the bottle. 'There, put it where it will do most good.' His hand stroked the hair back from her burning forehead. 'You are a poor old thing, aren't you? The best thing you can do is go to sleep and let the tablets do their work. It isn't a long flu. A couple of days will see you over it.'

He sat on the edge of the bed and went on stroking her head. It was both bliss and torture to Lauren.

'You'll catch my bugs,' she murmured, her eyes closing under his hypnotic touch, pushing her forehead puppy-like into the palm of his hand as he paused, in case he should taken her at her word and stop.

'No, I won't. I had this caper over Christmas.'

Her eyes flew open again. 'You were ill?'

'I told you I was cosseted, didn't I? My mother was in her element.'

Lauren hadn't realised that *that* was what he had meant. She had imagined something quite different.

'Did. . .did anyone else get it?' she asked.

'Everyone else stayed well away from me—until I was germ-free.' He was watching her carefully. 'A pity you didn't feel up to meeting my mother and Danielle this afternoon. Danielle brought her over to see the house, quite out of the blue. I would have liked to introduce you.'

'I would have liked to meet them,' she said politely. 'I just didn't want to intrude.'

He gave a snort of laughter. 'Liar! It sticks out a mile that you saw them arrive, panicked at the thought of meeting them, and bolted. You're a hopeless putter-on of acts.'

He was accusing her of not being able to pretend! That was rich when she'd spent weeks pretending her heart out! 'I put on a pretty good act of being your loving girlfriend,' she said crossly.

He looked steadily at her. 'I still say you're hopeless at putting on an act.'

There was a charged silence. Panic welled up in Lauren. 'I can't argue,' she said, finding that tears were rolling down her now hot cheeks. 'Oh, why am I doing this stupid crying business?'

'Because you're ill. I shouldn't have teased you. Go to sleep now.' He resumed his gentle stroking of her head. Sleep was safe. Sleep was desirable. Lauren's eyes closed. She wanted to tell him to go, but at the same time didn't want him to go. She wanted to stay like this for ever, his hand stroking her forehead. Either that, or she wanted to die.

It was eleven o'clock by her little bedside alarm when he roused her again to take more tablets.

'Four hours since you took the last lot,' he said bracingly. 'I've made some soup. Chicken. Guaranteed to restore strength and sanity. Will you give it a go?'

Lauren studied wearily. 'Maybe just a little.'

'Enough for a robin?' He grinned at her, then

stretched out one of her curls with his finger and let it spring back. 'Hang on to the intention. I won't be long.'

She went shakily to the bathroom and was glad to get back in bed again, refreshed by the quick wash she had had. Her clothes had been picked up, and there was a jug of juice and a glass by her bed. Tears stung her eyes again.

'Fool!' she told herself, and fought them back.

While she ate her soup, Charles sat in the cane chair and told her what she should do.

'You must take up that prize holiday of yours next week. It's exactly what you're going to need to get you fighting fit again.'

She looked balefully at him. 'What I'm going to need is a job. I haven't done a thing about getting one since New Year.'

'You'll be able to deal with that all the better for a holiday. In any case, it's surprising how things sort themselves out when you give them time.'

'I don't feel like doing anything at all.' She sank back on the pillows.

'You will in a day or two. After a holiday you'll move mountains.'

'In any case, it has to be taken in January. January's nearly over. And I'll never get a flight at such short notice.'

'What a Jeremiah you are! I'll make enquiries tomorrow. People are always open to suggestion.'

'I haven't said I intend going.'

'But you'll see the sense of it when the fever dies down,' he said with unshaken assurance. He picked up the tray. 'Now go back to sleep. I'll be here if you want anything.'

'I shall never sleep with you here.'

'You did very well for the past four hours. Snored like any old witch.'

'Oh-o-oh!' She buried her face in the pillow. 'I feel bad enough without you trying to make me feel worse!'

He put down the tray and sat in the chair so that his face was in her line of vision. 'You weren't really like a witch,' he said consolingly. 'More like Sleeping Beauty, in fact. And they were only the most kitten-like of snores. Does that suit the ego better? I'm staying because I want to make sure that you take the next lot of tablets. It's the only way to feel anything like comfortable, and you needn't object. It's your turn for a bit of cosseting. Now close your eyes, co-operate in the recovery schedule a little, and kindly go to sleep. I'm putting off the light now.'

Lauren lay, cocooned in the warmth of being looked after and the humour in his gently scolding voice. Her half-closed eyes focused drowsily on his dark, comforting outline until his shape blurred and she slipped into sleep.

Something roused her a little time later, and she found the chair empty. She had a strange, tingling feeling on her right temple. The sensation plagued her. The idea edged into her mind that Charles had kissed her there before going downstairs, and that was what had roused her. She touched the spot thoughtfully, oddly excited. Then reason stepped in. Why on earth would he kiss her when there was no one around to see? Kisses were for public consumption, not private pleasure. More likely than not she had awakened at the closing of her bedroom door.

She flung herself over and snuggled down under the duvet, warm, fed, cosseted. . .and disappointed, if she were honest, at this very moment. And certainly delirious, she thought hazily, trying to shake her mind free of its delusions. What tricks the imagination could play when assisted by a few flu bugs.

The sooner she got rid of this fever which put such lunatic ideas into her head, the better.

CHAPTER TEN

LAUREN took little notice of the take-off, staring absently out into the rushing air, her brooding brown eyes violet-shadowed. Charles had been so kind, so helpful, but in the end he had done so much to hasten her departure that it began to look as though he couldn't wait to be rid of her. And why not? The Roberta crisis was over. His house was furnished, and Danielle was smiling in the wings, waiting for the cue that would surely come to step on the scene and take centre stage. As for herself, Lauren reflected with rueful irony, she had what ought to be a comforting fat sum in her bank account for the work she had done at Longacre, but the comfort was far outweighed by the great big emptiness in her heart.

Be positive, she told herself. At least there was a fighting chance that the holiday would do her good, and she certainly needed to feel less limp before she went job-hunting. Her eyes focused suddenly on the dazzling skyscape all around and her heart lifted a little. There was sunshine up above the clouds. Perhaps her life too would find its sunshine. She hung on to the thought.

She was met at Point Salines airport by a tall, smiling Grenadian displaying her name on a big card. He was Carlton and he came with the house where she would be staying, he informed her, as did the car he was driving, and Renita, his wife, who was at home preparing a welcoming meal.

It was the start of the dry season. Warm air blew gently in Lauren's face as they followed the winding road, and there was lush, exotic vegetation conjured up by the rainy season on all sides. Carlton's warm,

happy voice pointed out landmarks, unwinding the
tension in her with its rich deepness. She rested her
head against the seat, eyes closed, face lifted to the
healing sun. She would enjoy these two weeks, she
vowed. It would be criminal to do otherwise.

They turned off the main road and went down an
unpaved tract through trees. When they emerged into
the bright sunlight again, Avalon was there before her,
making the breath catch in her throat, a white jewel of
an estate house surrounded by cherished lawns and
flowerbeds ablaze with hibiscus, bougainvillaea and
poinsettias.

'No estate now,' Carlton told her, going on in his
picturesque way of speaking, 'All sold, long time gone.
This old house ready to fall down, but new owner see
the ghost of beauty, and bring her breath again.'

Proudly he circled it in the car so that Lauren could
see the front and back verandas with their exquisite
lattice-work. When they came to the front of the house
again, Renita was waiting, beaming her welcome,
eager to shepherd Lauren through the lovely high-
ceilinged rooms as though she were visiting royalty.

The sea was a brief cliff path away, the beach a
curving private paradise edged with oleanders and
hibiscus through which Lauren could see crystal-clear
turquoise water creaming gently against shining white
sands. She kicked off her shoes and walked in the
shallows from one edge of the bay to the other,
breathing in pure, healing air, and marvelling that she
had almost not come to this wonderful place. If she
could regain strength for the future anywhere, surely
it was here.

She sat under a palm tree and watched the sunset
from her grandstand seat. Clouds dyed gold, flame,
pink and saffron surrounded the sinking sun. The sky
shaded from pale blue around the panorama in front
of her to almost black overhead. A golden path
stretched between sun and shore.

She wanted desperately to tell Charles how lovely it all was. The soft, rippling waves on the sand were making a noise that sounded like 'Bliss-s-s', but Charles was not here, and without his eloquent green eyes and haunting face it was not quite paradise.

She had forgotten how quickly night fell in the Caribbean. One minute she was watching a pageant of changing colours. The next, she was surround by utter darkness. But Carlton and Renita were taking care of her. Lights suddenly sprang into existence in the trees lining the path, and Renita's rich voice called, 'Missee Lauren! You come an' get it! Crab an' Calalloo soup waiting now!'

For the first time in days, Lauren felt hungry. She slipped on her shoes and called out that she was coming.

By the end of the first week it was a slim, golden-limbed Lauren who sat in her usual spot waiting for sunset. Her eyes and hair were shining with health, her body relaxed.

Carlton had driven her to all the island's beauty spots in the cooler hours of each day. Renita had cooked tempting island delicacies to spark her jaded appetite back to life, and every afternoon Lauren had swum and sunbathed or sought the shade on her private beach. Now, her white bikini had dried after her last swim, and she had knotted a black and white batik sarong skirt round her waist.

Tonight's sunset was particularly beautiful. As well as being flushed with colour, the billowing clouds massing on the horizon were edged with shining gold. Lauren gazed spellbound, her cushion propped against a palm tree. She was thinking of Charles, as she inevitably did when her heart responded to the island's beauty. She still missed him intensely, and so vivid were her thoughts of him that she even imagined that she heard his voice speak her name.

'Lauren!' It had happened again, but the sound was more real, more substantial this time. A footstep dislodged a stone on the cliff path, and she sprang to her feet, turned, and saw—actually *saw*—the subject of her thoughts. He was flesh and blood, no mental ghost, bronzed and smiling, in denim bermudas and white T-shirt.

Because his appearance was exactly what she had been yearning for, Lauren reacted instinctively to the fountain of joy that surged up in her. She flung herself into his arms, her face radiant, her voice jubilantly calling his name.

'Charles! It's you! You're real!'

His arms closed tightly around her and he laughed down into her glowing face.

'Something tells me that you're pleased to see me!'

'Completely bowled over! What are you doing here?'

'I wanted to see you,' he said simply.

The words sank into her mind. He wanted to see her. Charles wanted to see *her*. He had come *all this way* to see her?

'You've got business here?' Still she couldn't believe in the evidence of her ears.

He held her away from him, his hands gripping her shoulders, his eyes looking compellingly into hers.

'You could call it that. *You* are my business. And *this* is the nature of it.' He lowered his head and kissed her slowly, lingeringly, the touch of his lips dissolving the last trace of sadness in her, allowing joy to blaze in its place—joy that the one missing element in her paradise was at last here.

'Oh, I've missed you. . .' she said between kisses, clinging to him. Once she had begun to speak the truth to him, it seemed impossible to prevent it bursting out of her. 'I've been wishing every moment that you were here too.'

'And now I am.' His arms tightened round her

again, and she was drowning in his eyes, spinning away into a whirling heaven of sensation. This was the muscled strength of his body, hard and real against her softness, his lips warm and demanding on hers. Her arms locked convulsively round his neck and more happiness than she had ever known swept through her.

'I knew it was right for you to come here,' he told her softly. 'I knew that Avalon would work its magic and blow the past away.'

The present, full of its wonderful, inexplicable madness, was all she wanted. Charles' heart beating close to her cheek, Charles' arms warm and imprisoning. No past. No future. Simply now. But how long was 'now' going to last?

'How long are you here for?' she asked tentatively.

He looked into her eyes, smiling. 'As long as you are.'

'Where are you staying?' She was thinking of all the empty rooms at Avalon. Thinking, with uncharacteristic recklessness, of her own room. What wanton madness had been burned into her by the rays of the Caribbean sun?

He named a hotel a mile or so down the coast by the winding road. 'At least, that's where I'm booked in at the moment,' he said, with a look that sent the heady excitement bubbling up in her again. 'You can invite me to dinner here with you, though.'

'Of course.' The hours and days ahead shone like jewels, dazzling her. 'We'd better go and warn Renita. She's the housekeeper here. You'll love her.'

Night was falling with its usual startling suddenness. Charles took her hand in his and together they began to climb the path. But Lauren found it hard to tear herself away from a spot where such happiness had exploded in her. She lingered, pulling on his hand.

'Look at the moon rising. Isn't it beautiful?'

It was at her face, bathed in happiness and moonlight, that he looked as he said softly, 'Absolutely beautiful. . .'

She looked up at him, her eyes dark, glowing pools. A thought sent a ripple of anxiety to disturb them.

'Charles. . . I think I'm a little crazy right now. But not crazy enough to forget about Danielle.'

He paused, and the light of the lamp they were passing showed her that his expression was reassuring. 'We'll talk about Danielle later.' His hands cupped her face and he kissed her gently. 'Nothing to worry about. I promise. Just be happy and hang on to that.'

The car he had hired was in front of the house, and Renita was in the hall, ready to vet visitors.

Lauren, her face radiant with happiness, shyly introduced Charles. 'Renita, this is Charles Lennox, from England. Do you think you could make dinner stretch to two tonight? I know it's short notice.'

'You ever been short o' food?' Renita asked, arms akimbo.

'No! Of course not!'

Renita's eyes rolled in Charles' direction, full of humour. 'An' where dis friend from England staying?'

Charles named the hotel.

'What kinda cooks they got at yo' grand hotel?' she challenged.

'Good. But not as good as you, I'll be bound.'

There was a rich peal of laughter. 'You better say that, or you get no dinner. You both go sit you down. Can I stretch dinner? Well, yes, *oui*!'

Dinner was eaten on cloud nine. Lauren felt to be floating on happiness. Maybe she was mad, maybe she was a fool, maybe she had said goodbye to all reality, but the man she loved was sitting opposite her and he had travelled the width of the Atlantic ocean just to be with her. The knowledge was intoxicating. It drove out consideration of anything else. She would come down to earth with a bump, no doubt, but not now. Not glorious now!

Renita brought coffee out to them on the veranda.
Lauren told her and Carlton to go ahead with the visit
to the drive-in cinema at St George's, which she had
planned to make with them.

'Yo' friend from England goin' look well after you?'
Renita said, her eyes brimming over with laughter
again.

'You can count on it,' Charles told her firmly. 'Enjoy
the film.'

When they had driven away, he turned to Lauren.
'Now, my love. . .' he said, his voice husky and
intimate as he put his arm round her and pulled her
close. 'You and I must talk.'

'Must we?' Lauren murmured, clinging to him,
breathing in the familiar scent of his skin, rubbing her
cheek against the warmth of him, hearing the throb of
his heart. She didn't want to talk, she wanted to *be*.
She wanted this crazy magic that had her in its spell to
last for as long as it could. Talking called for thinking,
and thought destroyed magic.

'We have to. So much has been hidden, not said.
And there's been so much pretence. . .by me, as well
as by you.'

Lauren looked up at him, her attention caught at
last. He had been pretending?

'Down there on the beach, we both entered the
realm of the real at last,' he went on. 'For the first
time neither of us could either doubt or hide the fact
that being together was what we both wanted. Not for
work, not for any purpose other than the sheer joy of
being close to each other.'

His burning eyes demanded an answer. She nodded,
her own eyes lustrous with feelings she wanted neither
to deny nor hide.

'That feeling has been there from the start, I think,'
he said slowly, 'even when it was disguised by a
hundred and one other emotions. Why should I be so
angry about your seeming willingness to stay in a job

where you were being mercilessly exploited? Why
should it matter to me? I hardly knew you. . .and yet
something about you reached out to me and planted
the idea that you were important. . . One way or
another you were going to figure in my life.'

Lauren's finger traced the line of his lips. Her eyes
sparkled with mischief. His words thrilled her beyond
belief, but she couldn't resist teasing him. 'It didn't
seem like that when you found I'd got work in your
company. I seem to remember that you accused me of
wanting to exploit our acquaintance, Mr Lennox, sir!'

'Don't forget that I had some cause to be suspicious
of all women. It was what had gone before that spilled
over as suspicion of you.' He played with a curl of her
glossy hair. 'It wasn't long before I began to realise I
had a girl within reach whom I desperately wanted to
keep there. Someone I wanted to be far more than an
efficient working colleague to me. So——' The green
eyes assessed her reaction '—I arranged a weekend
which was ostensibly to sort out the problems of the
two of us working together. In reality it was to get to
know more about you, try to find out why you were so
distant to me as a person on the surface, when beneath
that level I sensed that you reacted to me in much the
same way as I did to you. When I knew about your
past, I realised that it wasn't going to be easy. I
couldn't rush you—that would be dangerous. But the
danger of losing you seemed everywhere. I was so
angry when you left Grenada, just as I was beginning
to think we were making a breakthrough. For the first
time you'd relaxed with me, then—wham! You were
off, and we were back to square one. That was when I
let the desperate desire to kiss you have its way, and
for the first time I think you admitted to yourself what
a wealth of feeling was waiting to flare into life
between us. . .and you couldn't get far enough away
from me. You couldn't take it. It was too soon.

So——' another assessing look '—I cooked up the Roberta affair.'

Lauren sat up suddenly. 'You mean that was a put-up job?'

'The situation existed, but of course I could have coped with it. The plain truth was that I wanted you near me, and enlisting your help seemed the best way of ensuring that.' His eyes glinted with devilment. 'Besides. . .it gave me such good reason to kiss you without your feeling that you had cause to be alarmed.'

'That's what you think!' Lauren said with feeling. She dived back into the shelter of his arms again and burrowed her face into his shoulder. 'Rehearsing, indeed! You made me feel. . .desperate!'

'I wanted to make you feel addicted!'

She sat up straight again and looked at him. 'What about the house?'

'Oh, that was perfectly genuine. Absolutely. But none of it achieved what I wanted to achieve. When we were alone, that awful ice age descended, didn't it? That was when I decided to resort to shock treatment. I'd succeeded only too well in convincing you that I was a disillusioned man who wanted no one. What if you thought I was beginning to want someone? Would jealousy shock you into being able to admit that you really did love me?'

Lauren raised her head to look at him, waiting breathlessly for him to go on.

His hand touched her face, caressed her cheek, slid gently down to rest in the curve of her neck. 'A glamorous-looking Christmas present, lovingly addressed, would start things off, I thought. Your subdued behaviour that night seemed to indicate that it had had its effect. If you only knew how I longed to own up when I took you home. . .' He twisted in his seat so that he could look at her. The movement set the hammock swinging gently. 'Well, now at last I can explain the inscription on the label. "Darling Danielle" is what my mother and father always called her. And "Charles-next-door" was her family's name for me as we grew up. So the label was merely one of our family in-jokes. Danielle's like a sister to me. I love her, dearly, but she isn't the girl I'm *in love* with.'

'Isn't she?' Lauren breathed happily.

'No, my credulous little idiot!' His tone made her dissolve with love for him. His kisses seemed to drink the essence of her. At last they came to earth again and she urged him to go on with his rewriting of their past.

'After Christmas,' he said, taking up from the point where he had been distracted, 'I played the photograph game. I scrounged that particular picture and frame from my mother—it's hers. Did all the moving around of it register?'

'It certainly did. You even took it into your bedroom. At least, I suppose that's where it was?'

'Go on! You looked!' He grinned delightedly at her, then the grin faded. 'All the same, it didn't exactly achieve miracles for me, did it? So I stepped up the pace. I thought perhaps if Danielle dropped in—unexpectedly—that might get you going. So I arranged that. And what happened then? *You* dropped *out* in all senses of the expression. That was when I decided that getting you over here, away from it all, was the only chance of working a little magic into our lives. And I was right, wasn't I?'

He took her in his arms. From somewhere an echo of unease drifted momentarily through Lauren's mind. Can it really be as easy as this? she asked herself briefly, before the heady reassurance of his kisses drove out thought.

Beyond the latticework of the balcony railings, fireflies danced. There was no man-made sound, only a piping chorus of tiny whistling frogs and the shrill chirping of crickets, and occasionally the rush of air overhead that marked the passing of a hunting bat.

Drunk on kisses, they at last pulled reluctantly apart and looked at each other. 'I'm not going to say anything more at the moment,' Charles said at last, cupping her face tenderly with his hands. 'I can't risk anything spoiling tonight. You still feel so incredibly fragile to me—like fine crystal, or butterfly wings—something that any careless move could destroy. More than anything I'd like to spend the night loving you. But before any such madness overtakes me, I'm going over to my hotel.'

'Must you?' Lauren found herself pleading unashamedly.

'For tonight, yes. But I'm leaving you with something which I hope will give you the security to ask me that same question again tomorrow, when my answer will be very different.' He kissed her lingeringly, then tore himself away again. 'Wait here.'

Lauren gazed with bemused eyes at the twinkling lights of a passing yacht, the continuing dance of the fireflies, the riot of exotic flowers where the lights of the house fell on them. Wonderland. She was Lauren in Wonderland. The dark tops of the trees surged violently in a sudden gust of wind, and she shivered. Wonderland was a figment of the imagination. Was the abrupt chill in the air an omen, or just a trick of the weather?

Charles came back.

'Wind's getting up. Only one of the night-time squalls, I think.' He put an envelope into her hand, a long, white envelope with her name written on it. 'I'm not going to explain this, because what's in the envelope says all I think you need to know. And now I'm going to leave you. But I'll be back tomorrow. And I hope you'll be able to tell me then what I want to hear. Until then, goodnight, my darling. Sleep well.'

'Goodnight, Charles.' Letting him go was unbearably hard. She hugged the envelope to her as she

watched him climb into his car, and stood waving until
the car disappeared from sight.

The wind was getting stronger. In a dream Lauren
went round the ground floor closing shutters, then
took the envelope upstairs with her. She wanted to
savour what Charles had written in the privacy of her
room. Already her heart was beating faster in anticipation of the words she would read. Words on paper
would anchor her to the earth, dispel this feeling of
unreality, convince her that this rainbow bubble she
felt to be in was the living, breathing world.

In her room she tore open the envelope and took
out the folded papers inside it. A fierce gust of wind
blew through the room. The shutters banged violently
back against the wall, then flew across the window.
Fate was playing games with her again. Frustratedly
she put the papers down and went over to secure the
catch, feeling again the chill in the air that she was
shutting out.

The papers had been blown off the dressing-table.
She picked them up, and sat on the padded stool, her
heart pounding as she unfolded them at last.

The chill in the air was nothing to the chill that fell
on her heart as she read. She had anticipated words of
love, but no words of love were there. Instead, as she
turned the pages, it was the cold jargon of a legal
document that confronted her.

Her house. He had bought her house in Cherwell
Terrace. He appeared to be giving it to her. It was
bought in her name. The convoluted legal language
was telling her so. She looked in the empty envelope.
There was nothing else.

The past and the present seemed to rush towards
each other, colliding with a sickening explosion that
shattered her dream.

Just like her mother. . . The words rang in her mind
like a death knell. She was being offered the same
cold-blooded deal as her mother had been offered. For

her mother a flat had been bought. And for her, a house. And Charles had thought that this transaction—for it was no more than that—was what she needed to convince her to become his lover. Not his wife.

She realised now that Charles had never in so many words spoken of the future—only of hoping to spend the rest of this holiday with her. In her company, and in her bed, he had implied. She was meant to feature in his life as one of his conquests, one of the girls with whom, as he had told her, he eventually exchanged an amicable farewell by mutual consent. She had been crazy enough to think he was leading up to telling her that he wanted her for life. And all he was offering her was this. . .this *pre-paid* arrangement for as long as the fancy took him, this ghastly repetition of her mother's story.

Numbly, moving as though in some dark dream, her world shattered, her limbs aching with a nightmare heaviness, she got out her case and packed her things. She crossed our her name on the front of the envelope, substituting his for it, then scored the word 'NO' in anguished capitals under it. When he came back tomorrow, he would find her gone. He would get the message, as she had got his.

When she heard the car with Carlton and Renita in it draw up, she went slowly downstairs, carrying her case.

'Now what happen?' Renita asked rouguishly. 'Don' tell me you go hotel too? This must be very good friend, oh yes, *oui*!'

'No, Renita,' Lauren said dully. 'I'm going home.'

The beaming dark face changed. 'You quarrel with friend from England?'

'I just have to go. I can't explain. I'm sorry. You've been so good. Will you take me to the airport, Carlton?'

'You got a flight booked?' Carlton asked, his kind face full of concern.

'No. I'll sort all that when I get there. I'm sorry to
drag you out again at this time.'

'No problem. Not for me.' Carlton's look of worry
intensified. 'You get in car, Miss Lauren. I need petrol.
Tank low just now.'

Lauren sat in the back of the car, her case on the
floor beside her, and waited numbly until Carlton
came out and topped up the petrol tank. Renita leaned
into the back of the car and enveloped Lauren in a
huge hug.

'Something sore in your heart, girl?' she said with
feeling.

Lauren nodded, unable to speak. Renita crushed
the bones of her hand with a violent squeeze and stood
back. Carlton got into the driving seat.

'You sure about this?' he asked over his shoulder.

'Quite sure.'

'OK.' He sighed. 'You're the boss.'

The car started up. The lights of the house faded,
and they swept through the dark trees. There was
nothing on the main road, only the twin beams of the
headlamps cutting through the darkness. Lauren was
barely aware of the slowing down after the first mile,
then Carlton was drawing to a halt beside a waiting
figure at the side of the road.

'Sorry, Miss Lauren,' he said as the back door was
opened and Charles slipped in beside her. 'Just didn't
seem good for you to go like that.'

'You were right to phone me, Carlton,' Charles said
grimly. 'Back to the house now.'

With Carlton sitting stiffly in the driving seat, able
to hear every word, Lauren sat in silence. The inevitable talking would begin soon enough. She felt numb,
almost anaesthetised. Fate was playing with her. Let it
play. It could do no more.

At the house, Carlton followed them anxiously into
the sitting-room.

'T'isn't right, all this pretending, Mr Charles,' he said with feeling. 'This young lady bin hurt by it.'

'You've done your bit, Carlton,' Charles said steadily. 'Now it's my turn. But you can get us a couple of brandies before you go.'

Lauren looked up bemusedly. Charles was giving orders and Carlton accepting with such easy familiarity. But why worry? Let it all happen.

He read her mind as he so often did.

'I suppose you're wondering why I'm giving orders to Carlton.' The green eyes looked levelly at her. 'The answer is that this is my house, of course, and Carlton and Renita have worked for me for years. If you hadn't run away from Grenada the first time, I should have brought you here then. If you wonder why the deception, try to imagine how I felt when you won the prize I had donated to the charity ball. How could I come clean about it? You wouldn't have dreamed of taking it up if it came from me, yet it seemed to me you damn well needed it. And you did win it fairly. I didn't rig the draw, if that's what you think.'

Lauren felt deadly tired. He was talking of trivialities. 'It doesn't matter,' she said. 'Nothing matters.'

Her white face and dead voice tortured him. With a muffled groan Charles threw himself down in front of her and gathered her hands into his.

'Don't *look* like that! Please, Lauren, darling, don't shut me out. Tell me what's upsetting you so much. I've done my level best to make it safe for you to allow yourself to love me. I thought I'd hit the solution of solutions with the house. I don't know how I've managed to devastate you like this.'

Lauren shuddered. Her hands were icy cold in his. She couldn't bear him to touch her. She pulled them away.

'Men always think money is the answer to everything,' she said, her voice lifeless. 'My father gave my mother a flat for as long as it suited him. He tried to

buy me off with money. You are just the same.' She
fell silent again. Charles' expression became alert. He
picked up on the least expected of her statements.

'Your father tried to buy *you* off? I didn't know you
had ever had contact with him,' he said carefully. He
sat on the chair at right-angles to the sofa where she
was sitting, not facing her, not too close. That was
better.

'Oh, we met.' She shivered. 'Nobody has ever
known. It wasn't the kind of meeting to want to
remember.'

'Tell me about it. Please,' he said softly. Then, more
urgently, he repeated, 'Please, Lauren.'

'It was a long time ago.'

'I still want to know. Tell me, please.'

She gave a shuddering sigh of resignation, too
exhausted to do other than obey.

'It was the holiday between A-levels and college. A
friend had moved to London with her family. I went
down to stay for the summer so that we could both get
holiday jobs in the city. I had good secretarial skills
already, and an agency sent me out to an office.' She
swallowed, her eyes huge and full of the past. 'I
worked there for three weeks before I realised that the
man who was my father worked there too.' She heard
his quick intake of breath. 'Yes. Ironic, wasn't it? But
it's the sort of trick that fate keeps playing on me. A
job in your firm. . . A holiday you've given. . . And
back then, a meeting with my father. He'd been on
holiday but he came back, and I watched him for three
more weeks before I told him who I was. He seemed
pleasant, ordinary. . . I told myself that perhaps he
had regretted what had happened. Maybe fate wanted
me to give him—give both of us—another chance.'
She swallowed convulsively. 'When I. . .introduced
myself, I thought he was going to die—have a heart
attack, a stroke, anything. When he could speak, he
said. . .he said, "I thought that problem had been

settled. What do you want? Money? How much will it take for you never to come near me again?" He thought I'd done it deliberately. Planned it all. Thought I was going to make some dreadful public scene in his place of work, maybe. Who knows? I—I left at once.' She looked eloquently at Charles. 'Sometimes the only thing to do in a situation is leave. Walk away from it.'

Charles half rose, and it was patently obvious that he meant to come over to her. Her hands gripped the cushions on either side of her, and she shrank back. He subsided into his chair again.

'Lauren. . .I can see why you wanted to get away from that particular situation. But I can't understand what made you want to leave me, now, without any response to what I gave you last night.'

Strangely, her strength seemed to be coming back. It was as though letting the poison of that brief meeting with her father out of its grave in her memory had freed her of its power. Her head lifted proudly.

'Can't you? It's simple. Neither my presence nor my absence can be bought. Something beyond money governs that.'

Protesting colour swept across his face. 'How can you say that after reading my letter? I'm not a man to indulge in honeyed words, but I bared my soul to you in that letter. Money was of the smallest relevance to what I thought was between us.'

'Letter? There was no letter. Just a legal document.'

He stood. 'Where is it?'

'On the tray over there.'

He stalked across the room, saw her message on the envelope and flashed an icy green look at her. He ripped open the envelope again and riffled through the pages of the contract.

'Well?' she said.

'Where did you open this?'

'In my bedroom.'

Another urgent stride across the room. He seized
her hand and tugged her to her feet. 'Show me!' he
said grimly.

In her bedroom, he looked round, to no avail. 'Tell
me exactly what you did when you opened it.'

'I sat here——' she sat on the dressing-table stool
'—I opened the envelope, expecting a letter. I looked
at the contents. . .' She remembered the chill that had
gone through the room. 'The wind banged the shutters. I went to close them, and when I came back, the
envelope and papers had been blown——'

Already he was tugging the dressing-table away from
the wall, reaching down behind it, standing up with a
look of triumph on his face and folded sheets of paper
in his hand.

'Here's your letter,' he said. 'Now perhaps you'll
read it.'

Lauren took it from him, a turmoil of feelings inside
her. She sank on to the bed, her eyes devouring the
bold, closely packed writing.

He had bared his soul, he said. It was true. His love
leapt from the pages, and before she had reached the
end tears were streaming down her cheeks.

The house was explained.

It seems to me that you have never had the
security of a place of your own, and that your
reluctance to entrust yourself to other people is
bound up in this, and in the unpredictability of the
people on whom you have had to depend. That at
least I can make up for. The house is yours, my
love. No strings, no conditions. It will always be
there, a secure place to return to. But what I hope
with all my heart is that from it you will be able to
emerge confident, secure and, above all, free to love
me as I love you. For you, I swear I would be
eternally predictable, totally dependable. And my
unconcealed hope is that you will one day soon want

to exchange this house for another, one which does come with strings and conditions: Longacre, which you have already furnished with loving care at my request, because who else should create the home but the woman who is to live in it? Longacre is waiting for you, my love. It can be yours. But for this exchange to be possible, you will have to become what I most dearly want you to become—my wife.

'Oh!' she cried painfully. 'How can you ever forgive me?'

He had been standing with his back towards her, staring out of the window. In an instant she was in his arms and he was looking down into her face while she sobbed out her pain incoherently. 'He bought a flat for my mother. I thought. . .I thought you were doing the same thing. And I had begun to believe you loved me. Oh, Charles! I hurt so much! And now I've hurt you! Can you forgive me?'

'I am not your father, who never forgave you for being born,' he said passionately. 'I'm the man who has never ceased rejoicing that you were alive from the moment he met you. There's nothing to forgive. I *understand*. The only thing I could never forgive would be your walking away from me.' He kissed the tears on her cheeks and eyes. 'Now,' he said with the utmost tenderness, 'are you going to change that "no" to the word I want to hear?'

Lauren clung to him fiercely for a moment, then turned a face that was radiant in spite of tears up to his. 'I think that all I ever wanted was to be allowed to love, and to be loved in return. These words——' she brandished the letter which she was still clutching '—these lovely words. . .they are what I really needed.'

Joy swept over his face. 'Then why, in the name of goodness, are you still crying?'

'Because I'm so utterly, incredibly happy!' she said, and laugher at her own jubilant, muddled explanation fought with her tears.

'That's better!' It was the managing director speaking, his voice triumphant, then dropping to a low, passionate tenderness. 'Now all you have to do, my love, is prove it!'

In the hall, Carlton and Renita, anxiously and shamelessly eavesdropping, exchanged delighted smiles and tiptoed away to their quarters. Nothing was more certain than the fact that they wouldn't be needed any more that night.

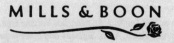

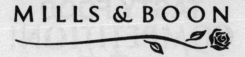

MILLS & BOON

Next Month's Romances

Each month you can choose from a wide variety of romance with Mills & Boon. Below are the new titles to look out for next month.

THE LAST GRAND PASSION	Emma Darcy
THE BALLEYMORE BRIDE	Emma Goldrick
THE SISTER SWAP	Susan Napier
SLAVE TO LOVE	Michelle Reid
BOND OF HATRED	Lynne Graham
MAIL-ORDER BRIDEGROOM	Day Leclaire
LACE AND SATIN	Helen Brooks
DANGEROUS PRETENCE	Stephanie Howard
IMPERFECT STRANGER	Elizabeth Oldfield
SEASCAPE	Anne Weale
PASSIONATE INHERITANCE	Rebecca King
A LITTLE CORNER OF PARADISE	Catherine Spencer
WICKED SEDUCTION	Christine Greig
PRACTISED DECEIVER	Susanne McCarthy
RELUCTANT DESIRE	Kay Gregory
DARK TEMPTATION	Joanna Mansell

TASTY FOOD COMPETITION!

How would you like a years supply of Temptation books ABSOLUTELY FREE? Well, you can win them! All you have to do is complete the word puzzle below and send it in to us by 31st October 1995. The first 5 correct entries picked out of the bag after that date will win a years supply of Temptation books (*four books every month - worth over £90*). What could be easier?

H	O	L	L	A	N	D	A	I	S	E	R
E	Y	E	G	G	O	W	H	A	O	H	A
R	S	E	E	C	L	A	I	R	U	C	T
B	T	K	K	A	E	T	S	I	F	I	A
E	E	T	I	S	M	A	L	C	F	U	T
U	R	C	M	T	L	H	E	E	L	Q	O
G	S	I	U	T	F	O	N	O	E	D	U
N	H	L	S	O	T	O	N	E	F	M	I
I	S	R	S	O	M	A	C	W	A	A	L
R	I	A	E	E	T	I	R	J	A	E	L
E	F	G	L	L	P	T	O	T	V	R	E
M	O	U	S	S	E	E	O	D	O	C	P

CLAM	HOLLANDAISE	OYSTERS	SPICE
COD	JAM	PRAWN	STEAK
CREAM	LEEK	QUICHE	TART
ECLAIR	LEMON	RATATOUILLE	
EGG	MELON	RICE	
FISH	MERINGUE	RISOTTO	
GARLIC	MOUSSE	SALT	
HERB	MUSSELS	SOUFFLE	

PLEASE TURN OVER FOR DETAILS ON HOW TO ENTER →

HOW TO ENTER

All the words listed overleaf, below the word puzzle, are hidden in the grid. You can find them by reading the letters forward, backwards, up or down, or diagonally. When you find a word, circle it or put a line through it, the remaining letters (which you can read from left to right, from the top of the puzzle through to the bottom) will ask a romantic question.

After you have filled in all the words, don't forget to fill in your name and address in the space provided and pop this page in an envelope (you don't need a stamp) and post it today. Hurry – competition ends 31st October 1995.

Temptation Tasty Food Competition,
FREEPOST,
P.O. Box 344,
Croydon,
Surrey. CR9 9EL

Hidden Question _____

_____

Are you a Reader Service Subscriber?   Yes ☐   No ☐

Ms/Mrs/Miss/Mr _____

Address _____

_____

_____ Postcode _____

One application per household.

You may be mailed with other offers from other reputable companies as a result of this application. Please tick box if you would prefer not to receive such offers. ☐

COMP395